THE

SILENT

STORM

THE

SILENT

STORM

Sherry Garland

HARCOURT BRACE & COMPANY

San Diego   New York   London

Requests for permission to make copies
of any part of the work should be mailed to:
Permissions Department, Harcourt Brace & Company,
6277 Sea Harbor Drive, Orlando, Florida 32887-6777.

First Harcourt Brace paperback edition 1995

Library of Congress Cataloging-in-Publication Data
Garland, Sherry.
The silent storm/by Sherry Garland.—1st ed.
p. cm.
Summary: Thirteen-year-old Alyssa has not spoken since seeing
her parents die in a hurricane, and now, three years later, another
storm threatens the home she shares with her grandfather on
Galveston Island.
ISBN 0-15-274170-4
ISBN 0-15-200016-X (pb)
[1. Orphans—Fiction. 2. Grandfathers—Fiction.
3. Mutism, Elective—Fiction. 4. Hurricanes—Fiction.
5. Galveston (Texas)—Fiction.] I. Title.
PZ7.G18415Si 1993
[Fic]—dc20 92-33690

Text set in Simoncini Garamond
Designed by Trina Stahl
Printed in the United States of America

B C D E F G
E F G H (pb)

To Joyce Schmitz—

oceanographer extraordinaire,

who has sailed at least four

of the seven seas

Acknowledgments

I would like to thank the following people for their generous assistance in providing information about hurricanes, shrimpers, and the flora and fauna of Galveston Island. I take full responsibility for any mistakes or inaccuracies that occur in the text.

First, special thanks to Dr. Robert E. Whitaker of Texas A&M University, Moody College of Marine Sciences; to the rangers at the Texas State Park at Galveston for information about beach ecology and hurricane effects on West End; and to "Bill," who so graciously allowed me to explore his shrimp boat. He, like the other shrimpers I spoke to, is a hardworking individual who is unlike Randon, the shrimp boat owner in this novel. Randon is a creation of my imagination and in no way reflects my impression of Gulf Coast shrimpers; nor is his character meant as a derogatory statement about this hardy breed of men.

And finally, I owe a big thank-you to Jake Fletcher for allowing me to use his computer to compose and revise this manuscript, and for getting me through the million and one computer problems I encountered along the way.

—S. G.

Contents

THE

SILENT

STORM

THE

DEVIL

WIND

Before the great storm that changed her life, Alyssa loved to hear tales about hurricanes and typhoons and cyclones. She would sit on the beach on a winter's night, huddled in the warmth of a crackling driftwood fire, listening to her grandfather tell stories about the cold North Sea near his native Scotland. Tales about violent, whirling maelstroms pulling ships and men to watery deaths; tales of sixty-foot waves rolling over decks and snapping masts in two. The screams of drowning sailors

1

filled her childish heart as she devoured each and every word the old sailor said about the seas he had loved and known all his seventy-five years.

Uncle D's stories were even greater. Uncle D was Alyssa's grandmother's older brother. During World War II, he had saved her grandfather's life after a German U-boat had torpedoed the Scotsman's merchant marine freighter. It was Uncle D who had pulled the wounded sailor from the icy waters and prevented him from losing his leg.

The two men became fast friends and after the war, Alyssa's grandfather visited Uncle D in his hometown of Galveston. The Scotsman—Bruce MacAllister was his real name, but everyone called him Captain Mac—fell madly in love with Uncle D's younger sister, a perky young nurse. They got married and lived on Galveston Island from that day onward.

Uncle D's side of the family had lived in Galveston for four generations. His stories were mostly about the Great Hurricane of 1900 that almost destroyed the city of Galveston, the worst natural disaster in American history. Of course, Uncle D had not been born until 1915, but he knew all about the killer storm that took more than six thousand lives, demolished over half the homes on the island, and ripped away large pieces of land. Both his father and his mother had been orphaned in that storm. They had seen their beautiful homes flattened into piles of bricks and wooden splinters and their parents' businesses washed away in a wall of seawater. And they had helplessly watched brothers and sisters screaming and dying, some drowned and some cut down by flying lumber and debris.

"A harrycane will pluck a palm tree up by its roots and send it scooting across the ground like a rolling pin. It'll snap telephone poles in two; it'll pick up a two-by-four and hurl it through a wooden wall like a javelin; or it'll push a fifteen-foot storm surge that floods everything in its path and carries waves that'll batter a building down to sticks." Uncle D's eyes would dim over and stare blankly out to sea when he talked like that, but Alyssa never wanted him to stop talking.

While other little girls asked to hear fairy tales of Cinderella or Sleeping Beauty or Snow White at bedtime, Alyssa begged to hear about storms at sea. She read everything there was in the library about hurricanes and fell asleep with her bed covered with tracking charts and photos of devastation by storms with names like Audrey and Beulah and Carla and Camille. She named her pet cat *Urican*, the word used by Indians of the Caribbean to mean "devil wind." And when her baby brother was born, she helped her mother pick a name—Dylan. It was the name of a Welsh sea god and meant "son of the waves."

When the horizon glowed crimson at sunrise and the pressure reading of the barometer hanging on a wall in her grandfather's living room began to fall, Alyssa's blood tingled in anticipation of the storm. The brighter the lightning, the louder the thunder, the more exhilarated she felt. Alyssa's favorite place was behind her grandfather's run-down horse stables near the beach, where she would stand spread-eagle while the wind whipped her clothes and the rain slapped her face. She would count the waves per minute and gauge their size, praying for a great storm to come during her lifetime.

Then one day Alyssa got her wish. The signs appeared and the great devil wind arrived in all its fury. It was just like the storms in the sailors' tales she had heard and the books she had read. Waves crashed, trees cracked, houses shattered, boats sank. And people died. But there was one thing that Captain Mac and Uncle D and all those books in the library had forgotten to mention—that the devil wind can tear families and people's lives apart just as it splits branches off a cotton-wood tree.

The floods recede; trees grow back; houses are rebuilt; and ships sail again. But a family destroyed is gone forever.

Maybe they had told Alyssa, and she just hadn't listened until it was too late.

Chapter One

THE

GREEN

BOAT

That steamy August morning would have been like any other except for two things: it was Alyssa MacAllister's thirteenth birthday, and she heard voices. Alyssa heard the voices long before she saw three shadowy figures sneaking through the marsh reeds along the finger-shaped cove that jutted into West Bay. The figures were searching for something, and in her heart she knew it was the green boat.

Alyssa was riding Stormy, her favorite horse,

as she did every summer morning. She loved to feel the misty morning air on her face and the wind whipping back her long, straight blond hair as she rode along the deserted beach on the west end of Galveston Island. Afterward she always crossed the narrow island to her secret cove. From there she would pole her green skiff out into West Bay and watch the sun rise over the end of the island.

As Stormy caught the scent of humans, he stuck his nose into the breeze as if to whinny. Alyssa quickly slid off and covered his soft gray muzzle with her hand. She led him to a patch of thick Bermuda grass and stroked his gray neck gently. Soon he was busy cropping the dark green blades and had forgotten the strangers.

Little ghost crabs scurried like shadows across her path as Alyssa crept along, trying not to stumble over the wild buttercups and tangy-smelling bindweed that covered the ground. They were on the leeward side of Galveston Island, so there were no big ocean waves. It was peaceful and quiet, except for the laughing sea gulls overhead and the soft lap of the inland waves from the bay.

As Alyssa sank into the shallow water, mud oozed over her sneakers and cold water soaked her socks. The pale yellow stalks of the reeds, which were the same color as her hair, and the wispy fog hovering over the marshes gave her perfect camouflage.

Alyssa knew her grandfather was going to be mad when he saw how dirty and wet she was. Lately he had been telling her that she was old enough to start acting like a young lady instead of a barefooted "heathern" with tangled hair and skin tanned as brown as a sailor's. He seemed to think she would suddenly start wearing dresses and fancy shoes and cut her hair when she turned thirteen. She supposed she was officially no longer a child, whether she liked it or not. But she didn't feel any older, so she had crept out of the house earlier than usual this morning to avoid hearing another lecture from the old man.

Alyssa tried not to think about what her grandfather would say. Right now, she had to find out what the three strangers were up to. Nobody had the right to be sneaking around in *her* secret cove.

As it grew lighter, the figures became clearer. One was tall, one was as round as a melon, and one was short and muscular, like a pint-sized boxer. They sounded like teenagers, but Alyssa couldn't see their faces clearly. She breathed slowly, trying to hear the intruders' words above the soft wind swishing through the cord grass and reeds.

"Ty," one of them shouted, "are you sure this

is where you left your boat? We've been looking for half an hour."

"I'm sure, Ernie. But like I told you already, it's a green boat and it's hidden in the reeds," the short one answered as he pushed aside one clump of grass after another.

A flash of anger exploded in Alyssa's heart. She clenched her fists and gritted her teeth to keep from leaping up and charging the thieves. How could that boy claim the boat as his? It had her name painted in large white letters across the stern; it was clean and well kept, not abandoned looking.

Alyssa squinted harder at the shadowy figures. If there had only been one boy, she would have taken him on. But three of them might mean trouble. If they would only separate, she could pick off the one left behind with the boat. Alyssa touched the slingshot that she always carried in her hip pocket in case she ran across a rattlesnake or a water moccasin.

A feeling of dread and helplessness washed over Alyssa as she watched the boys getting closer to her hidden skiff. She held her breath and crossed her fingers as the trio stumbled in the dim light. Suddenly the short one shouted in triumph. Alyssa's heart sank like an anchor.

She wanted to scream. She wanted to yell so badly that she began to tremble all over. But when she opened her mouth, her throat suddenly grew tight as if a hand of steel had squeezed around it. Her heart pounded with a familiar sense of dread as it always did when she tried to speak. She felt as if something terrible, something horribly unspeakable was about to happen. It had been that way ever since the day of the great storm three years ago—the day her parents' charter boat went down at sea.

Nausea rolled over Alyssa as a quick jolt of memory rushed toward her. She saw high waves, slanted rain, a sinking boat. And there was something else, something just out of her memory's grasp. Her lips formed a word, but as she struggled to speak, the fear and dread swept over her like a wall of seawater.

Alyssa swallowed and squeezed her eyes shut. The sensation would pass. It always did whenever she decided not to speak. Breathing slowly, she counted to ten, then opened her eyes.

She saw the short boy pulling her boat from the reeds. It was a flat-bottomed skiff that she could stand up in and pole over the marsh flats or sit down in and paddle through deeper water. It was perfect for flounder gigging or trolling. Her father had made it with his own hands for her tenth birthday. That had been two weeks before the tropical storm destroyed his charter boat and

11

carried him off to sea. But Alyssa didn't want to think about that day, so she forced thoughts of the storm out of her mind and strained to hear the three boys.

"What'd I tell you," the short one said as the other two sloshed out to join him.

"Hey, man, this is great. Sorry I ever doubted you, Ty," the tallest one said. Then he turned to the round boy. "Hal, go get our fishing tackle. Let's get started before the sun gets up too high."

"Ah, man, why do I always have to do the dirty work?" the chubby boy complained. He crossed his arms and dug the toes of his sneakers into the damp sand.

" 'Cause I'm older," the tall one said in an angry voice. "Now stop whining. The wind's picking up. Pretty soon we won't be able to fish."

"Ah, man . . ."

"Look, I'll let you use my new fishing rod for a while, okay?"

"Oh, okay. But I'm not lugging your stuff around for the rest of the day like I did last time."

The stocky boy muttered under his breath as he stomped past Alyssa's hiding place, kicking up silver flurries of sand. She recognized him from junior high. He often hung around the halls or in the lunchroom, messing around with some other boys. She thought he might be the guy who had turned her bowl of chili upside down one day when she got up to get more crackers. Or he might have been one of the kids who called her "crazy" or "mental case" or "Looney Tunes." They didn't think she could see them staring at the black-tinted windows of the van that carried the Special Ed students, but she could. A lot of the kids thought that just because Alyssa couldn't speak, she couldn't hear, either. They talked about her as if she weren't there. And sometimes, she wished she *couldn't* hear.

Hal was so close to Alyssa she could have grabbed his foot. She started to trip him but stopped. It would only make the other boys come running. Her best hope of saving her boat was for the three to separate.

As Alyssa watched Hal stomp by, hot tears filled her eyes and a deep fury built inside. She hated what was happening. If she could just talk like a normal person, maybe all she would have to do was stand up and explain that the boat was hers. But she knew she couldn't talk, and she had left her grandfather's house in such a hurry that she had forgotten the little notepad and pencil she usually carried. In frustration, she gritted her teeth and clenched the pale yellow stalks until they bent in two.

As Alyssa waited, she thought about the way her father had looked the day he gave her the flat-bottomed skiff. He had grinned and laughed while she leapt in and out of it. The air that day had smelled fresh and damp from an early morning rain, and the sun made everything glisten like silver and pearls. Day and night, they explored around the bayou and other coves up and down West Bay. They found secret hidden channels that nobody knew about and little spaces and trails made by waterfowl. They caught flounder and redfish for three days in a row and had planned to go gigging at night as soon as the moon had phased out. But that day never came for the two of them.

Even after three years, Alyssa couldn't believe that her father was gone. She couldn't shake the feeling that he was still somewhere on the island. After all, his body had never been found. Didn't that mean there was still a chance he was alive? Maybe he had hit his head and suffered from amnesia, like in the old black-and-white movies they used to watch on the late, late show. He might be working down at the docks, not knowing who he was. Maybe someday he would show up on Captain Mac's doorstep as if nothing had ever happened. Not a day passed that Alyssa didn't think of where he might be and what she would say when he came back. And in every daydream, she *knew* that the moment she saw him she would speak again.

By now the other two boys had hold of the long towrope and were dragging the green boat from its hiding place. They hauled it up onto the shore, then began playing around and fighting over who would get inside first. Alyssa swallowed her anger and began to move.

While the boys wrestled, Alyssa inched closer through the shallow water, being careful not to stir up any water moccasins or step on a stingray. Normally she wouldn't wade without rubber boots and lots of light—she had seen enough wounds to know that going barefoot or wearing thin sneakers like her own was foolish—but at the moment she wasn't using common sense. Only her boat mattered.

After getting as close as she could, Alyssa squatted down in the two-foot-deep water until the tips of her long hair floated on the dark surface. She shivered, but whether it was from being cold or scared or mad, she couldn't tell.

The boys soon dropped to the dirt, huffing and puffing. Even though they were on the lee side of the island, a steady breeze blew back their hair and whipped their T-shirts.

"Why's it so windy this morning?" the short one named Ty asked.

"Hurricane Berta's coming. Don't you watch TV?"

"Our TV's busted at the rent-house. And we don't have one on the shrimp boat. I reckon my stepdaddy knows about it, though."

"Well, Channel Two says it may hit Texas in a couple of days. They think it's going to hit south of here, close to Corpus Christi. But they can't say for sure yet. At least it'll cool off for a while. I can't stand this hot, hot weather much longer."

Alyssa slipped her hand over her mouth to keep from chuckling. Anybody with a lick of sense could tell that a hurricane was coming. All they had to do was watch the signs in front of their eyes. The sea level was rising—the very spot where she was hiding had been no more than damp sand two days ago. And the waves from the ocean were different—big, slow, undulating combers that she could see rolling all the way from the horizon—instead of the usual breakers. Just warning messages from Hurricane Berta that she was going to pay a visit.

The animals knew something was going to happen. Gulls and terns and rabbits were acting nervous. Snakes were crawling to higher ground. Even her grandfather's horses, as old and tame as they were, would roll their eyes and spook at the slightest noise and paw the sand in their stalls.

"Great! Just great!" Ty yelled as he punched the wind and snapped his hair back with a toss of his head. "The last week of summer vacation and a stupid hurricane has to come and blow us away. It ruins all my plans. Shoot!" He sighed. "Well, I guess we'd better fish like crazy while we can."

"You're right. Tonight we'll probably pack up and leave the island until the storm passes. My mom gets hysterical when it comes to hurricanes. How about your folks, Ty?"

The short boy shrugged his sturdy-looking shoulders. "Ah, my stepdaddy don't care. We live on the shrimp boat half the time during the summers anyhow. He just heads up the river channel or takes the boat up the coast to a safe port. He's probably halfway to Louisiana right now."

"Bull! He wouldn't go off and leave you behind."

"Sure he would. He did it before. And he never even missed me until it was time to haul up the nets and snap off the shrimp heads. Ah ... forget it, Ernie. It don't matter anyhow. Say, what's taking your brother so long?"

The boys turned to the east, and so did Alyssa. The orange-red ball of fire climbed over the tip of the island, casting an eerie tint over the cold, gray sand and on the white wings of the sea gulls. Across the bay, car headlights flickered on the causeway as commuters drove to Houston or to the oil refineries of Texas City, whose pale yellow lights twinkled in the brownish haze.

Alyssa sieved the sand and clay near her feet through her fingers until she felt some pieces of shell. She put a handful in her pocket, then slipped a piece into the leather pouch of her slingshot. Carefully she drew it back and aimed at the tall boy. A loud shout made her stop.

"What was that?" Ernie asked as he jerked his head around.

"Sounded like Hal."

The sound came again, this time clearly a boy's squeaky voice.

"Ernie, Ty! Over here! Come see what I found."

Ernie and Ty leapt up and ran toward the open fields.

Alyssa sloshed out of the water reeds and ran to her green boat. She leaned over and kissed the prow, as if it were a child, then dug her feet into the cool mud at the bottom of the cove and yanked on the towrope. From behind her came the shouts and squeals of the boys and the neighs of a horse.

Over her shoulder, Alyssa saw the boys struggling with Stormy. For a moment she wrestled with her decision, but she knew what had to be done. Stormy could take care of himself. He could kick and bite and run, but a boat was at the mercy of whatever hand pulled its rope. Quickly Alyssa tossed in the rope, jumped inside the boat, and began poling down the bayou toward the deeper water of the bay.

When the water was about three feet deep, she sat down and rowed the skiff as fast as she could toward the mouth of the bayou, about twenty yards away. From there she could go out into West Bay and get away from the boys. Even though they might follow her, she doubted they would take the chance of going out very far. Her small, hard muscles tightened as the paddle hit the water faster and faster.

"Hey, you, stop! Come back here with my boat!" the short boy screamed from the shore.

The boys waved and ran and shouted. They splashed out into the cove, stirring up mud and sand, but stopped near the spot where the water turned darker. Normally wading out into the cove or the bay was easy, but the approaching storm had raised the water level an extra two feet. At least the boys had enough sense to not follow her.

Now the boys were running along the edge of the bayou, waving frantically as if they were losing their most prized possession.

"We've got to stop her," Ty shouted as Alyssa reached the mouth of the bayou and started for the bay waters.

"She's too far out. The water's four or five feet deep, and I'm scared of the current," Ernie yelled back.

Alyssa smiled when she saw them chug to a stop. Ty was talking to the tall boy, but she couldn't hear what he said. Ernie seemed to protest, then turned around and trotted away. Ty cupped his hands over his mouth and called to Alyssa.

"Hey, you, Blondie! We've got your horse. You'd better bring that boat back here or you'll be sorry."

Alyssa stopped paddling. There in the flats stood Ernie and Hal, leading Stormy by his halter rope. Anger swelled up inside Alyssa. She opened her mouth to yell, but as usual the steel fingers gripped her throat and panic and dread swept over her. She shook her head and slammed her fist against the side of the green boat.

Ty waded out toward Alyssa until the water sloshed against his thighs. He had a smug smile on his lips, as if he'd just won a bet. Reluctantly Alyssa paddled back toward the shore to meet him. Stormy could probably take care of himself, she thought, but he was an awfully friendly horse. He trusted people too much, especially children and teenagers. He would lose his head for a piece of bread. Alyssa couldn't bear the idea of leaving him with the boys, so she gently poled the skiff until it was only a few feet from Ty in the shallow bayou waters.

In the early light she could see his features clearly. Shaggy, dirty blond hair flopped into eyes as blue as morning glories. And he was even shorter than she had imagined. But his arms and shoulders rippled with muscles, and his hands were hardened with calluses from hard work. She supposed he was cute, in a way, but she had never trusted cute boys.

"Bring that boat closer, Blondie," he said as he reached for the towrope.

Alyssa slammed the paddle down on his knuckles.

"Oww!" he screeched, and jerked back his hand.

As Ty tried to grab the boat again, Alyssa smacked the oar down on his back. It popped even louder than his knuckles had.

"Watch out, Ty," the boy named Hal shouted from the shore. "That girl's crazy. Everybody at school calls her Looney Tunes. She's always fighting other kids and getting into trouble. She bites like a dog. Don't you, Looney?" He pointed a chubby finger at her.

Alyssa glared at his freckled face. With a squeak in her throat, she brandished the long pole like a spear, then hurled it at him. It just nicked the side of his leg as he jumped out of the way. Ty tried to pick up the paddle at her feet, but Alyssa quickly grabbed the other end.

"Let go," Ty muttered between clenched teeth. "Come on, skinny, let go!" Ty braced his short legs, then jerked the oar with all his strength.

Alyssa felt her body being lifted off the seat and then falling, but she was determined not to let him have the paddle. Water flooded over her head and filled her mouth as she landed on her stomach. When she sat up, Ty had a funny look in his eyes.

"Hey, I'm sorry," he said. "I didn't mean to knock you in the water. You shoulda let go, for Pete's sake." He reached for her arm.

That was what Alyssa wanted. She spat a stream of water into his eyes, kicked his knees, and flailed her arms until a wall of white spray deluged him. Ty covered his eyes with one hand and tried to grab Alyssa with the other, but it was too late. She was up on her feet. She slapped his chest with a loud pop and watched Ty land on his behind in the shallow water.

Staggering out of the cove, Alyssa felt Ty's hand brush against her ankles as he tried to seize her feet. She gave a little kick, then ran toward the dry sand flats, dripping a river of water and collecting a mountain of sand on her wet shoes.

"Ernie, stop her!" Ty shouted to the tall boy holding Stormy.

But Alyssa wasn't worried about Ernie. She stopped long enough to remove a piece of shell from her pocket, slip it into her slingshot, and aim at the tall boy's chest. The shell zinged through the air and hit him on the shoulder. Ernie winced and yelped, but he didn't let go of Stormy's halter rope. Alyssa suddenly remembered a trick she had taught the gray horse. She put her fingers to her lips and released a loud, sharp whistle.

Stormy straightened his ears. He reared high, pawed the air, and let out his most threatening squeal. How could anyone be afraid of that sweet gray face and those gentle brown eyes, Alyssa thought. But she was glad that Ernie dropped the rope and panicked as if he were being attacked by sharks.

With a running leap, Alyssa was up on the gray mustang's back. She spun Stormy around, then dug her heels into his flanks.

"No!" Ernie cried when he heard Stormy's hooves thundering down the sandy trail.

For a moment, Alyssa struggled to keep her balance on the wet, bare back. She leaned down low and grabbed a hank of mane. The wind whipped back her long, wet hair, but it did not cool her flushed face.

"I told you she's nuts," Hal whined as he joined the other two running boys.

"Where are we going?" Ernie asked.

"Follow me," Ty shouted back.

The words were hardly out of his mouth as he charged into the bay and sloshed out toward the deeper water. The other two boys followed him in, just as Stormy reached the water's edge. Alyssa urged the small horse into the water. He high-stepped as if he were enjoying himself and churned the water to a muddy brown color. The boys kept swimming out until they were in water about four feet deep. Alyssa shot pieces of shell at them with her slingshot until she ran out of ammunition. Then she slid off Stormy and picked up the green boat's towrope.

"Hey, what are you doing, Looney Tunes?" Ernie yelled. "That ain't your boat."

Alyssa pointed to the name on the stern, then thumped her chest. Ernie broke into laughter.

"Oh, I see—she Tarzan," he mocked, then

beat his own chest and let out a Tarzan yell. Hal laughed, but Ty didn't join in.

"What are you trying to say, Blondie?" he asked. "Why don't you speak up?"

Alyssa opened her mouth, determined to speak this time, no matter how painful her throat felt. She had already chosen the words she would say: "This is my boat. You can't use it." But as she moved her lips, the awful fear rushed over her. She began to shake. The sound was in her throat and her tongue was willing, but the noise would go no farther than her voice box. Her vocal cords vibrated a second, then she slammed her fist against the boat. She knew she would not speak this time, either.

Alyssa hated herself for being so afraid of something that she could not even see or touch. Her father would have called her a coward for being so scared. The thought of disappointing him made her even more frustrated, and she hit the boat again.

Still out in the bay, Ernie and Hal cackled and imitated her guttural noises, but Ty remained quiet.

Hot tears filled Alyssa's eyes, and she turned away so the boys would not see her cry. She loosely wrapped the end of the towrope around Stormy's chest, then climbed onto his back. As he began walking, the little green boat glided out of the water onto the shore.

"Come back with Ty's boat!" Hal shouted. Ernie joined in, and they both hurled curses and insults at Alyssa's back. She had no intention of turning around until she heard someone sloshing out of the water and chuckling. She couldn't resist peeking over her shoulder. She saw Ty standing on the shore, shaking his head like a dog in the rain and wringing out his Batman T-shirt. He looked like a midget compared to tall Ernie, who had stepped up beside him.

"What a girl!" Ty half yelled, half laughed.

Ernie swung around to face his short friend, his hands on his hips and a scowl on his face.

"Don't you mean to say, 'What a looney'?" Ernie asked.

"Well," Ty said, "if she's crazy, then what does that make us? She's got the boat and she's got the horse, and all we've got is wet britches."

Then Ty flashed a smile and waved at Alyssa.

"Bye-bye, Blondie! Have a nice day!" he called.

Alyssa hated herself for having one good thought about the guy who had tried to steal her boat, but she couldn't stop the little smile that crept to her lips. And she couldn't resist waving back to him before clucking to Stormy and riding away.

As Stormy picked his way across the fields, dragging the green boat, the boys' shouts faded away. Alyssa wasn't the superstitious type: she never believed in the danger of black cats or walking under ladders and such. But it was her thirteenth birthday and already things were going wrong. She couldn't shake the feeling that the rest of the day, and maybe even the rest of her life, was going to be just as unlucky.

Chapter Two

CAPTAIN

MAC

As Stormy followed an old, narrow road lined with cattails and palmettos, Alyssa thought about what the boy Hal had said. He was right about her problems at school. Each year got worse, but last year—the year she had to repeat sixth grade—had been the worst of all.

Alyssa had not always hated school. She had enjoyed doing homework and studying for exams when her mother was alive. But her grandfather showed no interest in helping her. He couldn't see well enough to read her books. And being a Scotsman, he didn't know a lot about American history and government. He could recite a long list of British kings and queens and told his grand-daughter about the War of the Roses. He knew most of Robert Burns's poetry by heart. But that sort of information never came up on her exams. Neither did the names of the parts of ships, nor the fastest routes across the seas, nor the patterns of hurricanes.

More than anything else about school, Alyssa hated the tests the nurses and psychiatrists gave her to find out why she couldn't speak. They were always probing and prying and asking questions that were none of their business.

It wasn't that Alyssa didn't want to speak. She tried, *really* tried. Sometimes the words wanted to get out so badly she hurt. But something in her throat always locked up and nothing could get out. She felt as if her words were prisoners down in her belly, guarded by a steel door with latches and chains. And nothing could break those bonds, especially not the psychiatrists and their endless questions.

Sometimes she dreamed she was screaming. Often she awoke with a throbbing, raw feeling in her throat and found her cat staring at her with a puzzled expression on its face.

Alyssa *did* agree with one thing the doctors said. If she could just remember what had happened on the charter boat the day it sank, she was sure she would get well and speak again. But no matter how hard she tried, she could not recall how she got on her parents' boat that stormy day, or why she was there, or why she was the only passenger in the lifeboat when it crashed ashore. Nor could she remember the circumstances of her mother's death, or why her father had disappeared without a trace.

Whenever she did try to dredge up memories of that day, Alyssa developed an agonizing headache and her stomach turned over. It was as if a monster were caged in the back of her brain. If she so much as tippy-toed toward that cage and peeked in, the memory monster would roar and scare her so badly she would shake all over.

No matter what the doctors told her, she could not stop feeling that the accident that day was in some way her doing. Perhaps she had caused the motor to stall out somehow. Maybe she had gotten hysterical and caused her mother to drown or knocked her father overboard into the raging sea. How else could she have ended up being the only one in the lifeboat? Even though she could not remember what had happened, in her heart she *knew* it had been her fault. After all, wasn't she the one who had prayed for a hurricane?

As Stormy crossed Termini Road, the county road that ran the length of the west end of the island, Alyssa smelled tangy weeds and grasses and the salty, fishy scent of the ocean surf that roared ahead of them. Hardly any traffic moved on the road at that early hour. And most of the vacationers had left to avoid the approaching hurricane. A few fishermen in old pickups chunked along, probably on their way to San Luis Pass for some wade-fishing before the storm.

Half a mile down the road, to her right, houses rose high off stilts in Pelican Village. That was where Alyssa and her parents had lived before the accident. To her left, mists rose from empty pastures and low marshes. White cranes picked at the mud and a great blue heron suddenly flew off with loud, angry screams. It flew so low, the wind from its wings stirred the calm black waters. A few miles farther to her left, the dim outline of tall condominiums rose into the morning sky.

The green boat scraped across the asphalt road, then thumped onto a sandy trail that led down to the beachfront. The only sounds came from the sea gulls overhead, the pounding surf, and the wind. The three boys had been right about one thing. The wind velocity had gradually increased since yesterday. The weather service had already issued small-craft advisories all along the Gulf Coast because of choppy seas.

After a few minutes of riding down the beach toward the rising sun, Alyssa arrived at her grandfather's run-down stables poised on the edge of a small pasture about ten yards beyond the sand dunes. Not far from the stables, her grandfather's little house stuck up on heavy wooden pilings. It was really more of a shack, with its weathered gray wood siding, its loose shingles, and its sagging concrete porch steps. The yard fence had long ago fallen down and succumbed to rambling bindweed and purslane vines. The only color in the yard came from beds of giant zinnias and periwinkles and purple bachelor buttons. Alyssa's mother had planted them many years ago, and they came up each spring with no help from anyone. Along the side of the stables a big clump of red cannas had grown so tall that they covered up one window. Alyssa tried to keep all of the plants weeded and watered in the hottest of summer when they usually wilted, as a memorial to her mother.

Alyssa smiled as she pictured her trim mother, always busy working in the garden, her knees and hands covered with earth. She could save any plant, no matter how dried up and hopeless it looked. Alyssa missed her terribly, but at least she knew where her mother was. A beautiful white stone angel guarded her grave on the other end of the island. The double headstone had her father's name inscribed on it, too, but Alyssa knew that was wrong.

Whinnies filled the air as small horses poked their heads over the tops of stall doors. Out front an old sign danced on squeaky hinges. Its faded letters read Horses for Rent. No wonder business had fallen off for the past three years, Alyssa thought, as she glanced at the stables and house. Most tourists probably thought the place was closed down, or they couldn't read the rusty sign.

Alyssa left the green boat in the sandy backyard and led Stormy to a stall that had his name painted in crooked red letters above the half door. Empty stalls enblazoned with faded names like Dondi and Spanky and Pogo stretched to the end of the stable. During the late 1940s and in the 1950s, not a single stall had stood empty. Captain Mac had even owned a small restaurant and dance pavilion back then. Many of his customers were tourists visiting the fancy gambling boats at Galveston's port. Even famous movie stars dropped in at the stables for moonlit horse rides.

Alyssa's father had been a little boy when he met Lana Turner and she asked him to ride with her. He must have told Alyssa that story a hundred times. The horse ran like the wind as the waves crashed against its hooves, and the salty seafoam sprayed into the little boy's face while the beautiful actress hugged him tightly.

An empty feeling crept into Alyssa's heart and a big lump choked her throat, as it always did when she thought about her father's wonderful stories. Sometimes he had talked for hours while they were fishing. He told her stories about winning the state baseball championship when he was in high school, or catching his first flounder, or how he met her mother.

Alyssa lifted the metal feed bin and scooped out a bucket of grain and oats and poured the mixture into Stormy's trough. She repeated the chore for the other six compactly built horses that occupied one side of the stable. Like Stormy, they were all mustangs—small, sturdy descendants of those first horses left behind in the southwestern United States by Spaniards more than four hundred years ago.

Alyssa flipped on the portable radio and tried to listen to the music while she cleaned out the stalls and tossed in fresh hay. When the weather report came on, the deejay announced the latest coordinates for Hurricane Berta. It was still heading slightly toward the southern part of Texas someplace near Corpus Christi, but no one could say for sure if it would recurve and veer to the north. It happened all the time, depending on what kind of weather was hovering over the mainland. Even if the storm didn't hit Galveston, the cooler, wetter weather would be a welcome respite from the scorching ninety-two-degree days they had been suffering through for the past weeks.

Alyssa stuck a red pin to mark the longitude and latitude of the storm on a tracking chart that she'd tacked to the stable wall. She had cut it from the back of a brown paper grocery sack earlier that month and had been tracking the storm for eight days now, since its birth in the Atlantic. Overnight Berta had been upgraded from a category two to a category three hurricane. It wouldn't be the worst to hit the Gulf coast, but still its winds could be devastating. If it hit to the west of the island, Captain Mac's house and stables would be flooded by the storm surge and maybe destroyed by the wind and waves. If the storm hit to the east of the island, it wouldn't be as bad because the wind would push the ocean waters away from them.

After the horses finished eating, Alyssa led them into the small fenced-in pasture that served as a corral. Weeds and stickers grew profusely around the edges, but there was enough Bermuda grass to keep the horses interested. After combing some burrs out of Stormy's black tail and mane, Alyssa returned to the tack room and took out some bridles and saddles, just in case a rare customer stopped by.

A car door slammed from the direction of the gravel driveway. Then Alyssa heard the familiar voice of Uncle D greeting her grandfather. After her great-uncle had gone inside the house, Alyssa hooked up a garden hose to the water hydrant under the kitchen window. She stretched it to the corral and filled a large galvanized tub. While she rewound the hose, she heard the two old salts' voices drifting through the open window and back door. But there was none of the usual bickering, arguing, and calling each other names or slapping knees as each one tried to outlie the other.

It was far too quiet inside. She heard the steady drum of the waves against the beach and the buzz of a fat horsefly trying to get out through the rip in the back-porch screen door. Something was wrong. Alyssa sat at the top of the concrete steps and pressed her ear to the tattered screen. She stroked her cat, Urican, absentmindedly as it curled up in her lap.

"Well, Mac," Uncle D said, "maybe the harrycane's gonna miss Galveston this time. What do you think?"

"It doesna' matter, Davy." Alyssa's grandfather spoke in a heavy Scottish brogue that other people often did not understand. "I canna survive even a wee hurricane. These old legs ha' finally withered away to sticks. Do ye not know how painful it is just to walk aboot the house? I canna even fetch mail from the box. If it weren't for Alyssa, the wee horses would be starvin'. They canna depend on the likes o' me na' more."

"Posh! You're just getting lazy, Mac."

"Nay, what I'm gettin' is homesick for the Highlands. I want to go back to Scotland before it's too late. I've still got a sister there."

Alyssa's stomach lurched and her heart skipped a beat. Her grandfather only talked about going back to Scotland when he was very depressed. At times like that he would tell her that he wanted to die there and be buried beside his parents in the family cemetery. Alyssa didn't understand why he didn't want to be buried next to her grandmother, who had died of cancer many years ago. And she wondered how Captain Mac could even think of moving away when her father, his own son, Robbie, might come back someday. Alyssa hoped that it was just a spell of what he called "the doldrums." But when the old man spoke again, there was something in his voice that made Alyssa hold her breath.

"I *am* movin' away this time, Davy. I'm sellin' the horses, too. They're gettin' old, like me. The profits keep gettin' smaller every year. Face it, man, nobody wants to ride horses na' more. They've got dune buggies and motor bicycles nowadays. It'll never be like the grand old days when fine lads and lassies rode the horses in the moonlight."

"Oh, hush up, Mac. You've been whining for years about your galderned legs and the business—every time a little harrycane brews up in the Gulf. You'll ride this one out, just like all the others."

"But I'm na' kiddin' this time, man. I'm tired. Tired of everything around here. It's too painful to look at this place anymore. It's so lonesome without my Robbie and Phyllis. I don't know how I've held on these past three years without them. I want to smell the heather one more time before I die." He heaved a long, ragged sigh.

"Die? You're too ornery to die. And what about your granddaughter? What about Alyssa? Answer me that, Bruce MacAllister."

"Aye, there's the biggest rub. The lass is gettin' worse and worse. The doctors thought she might start talkin' anytime. Elective mutism caused by the trauma of seeing her parents killed, they said. Nothin' physical wrong with her wee throat. But it's been three years. Three years!" He thumped his cane on the wooden floor.

Alyssa scooted closer to the door, leaning into it. She swallowed hard and felt sneaky for listening to their conversation. But she couldn't pull herself away. Not now.

"Her schoolmaster says she's gettin' farther and farther behind in her learnin'," Captain Mac continued. He sighed, then banged the table, making the utensils clatter. "The lass isn't stupid. She's as bright as the mornin' star, that one is. She just won't study or do her lessons. Just sits and looks out to sea half the day. Doesn't have nary a friend at school or home. And always gettin' into fights and such. The Good Shepherd knows I've tried to make her open up, but she's closed as tight as a clam."

"She'll open up someday, Mac. You know it and I know it. The child just needs time to forget," Uncle D said in a calm voice.

Alyssa wanted to run inside and hug his old, stooped shoulders in thanks for the kind words. But Uncle D was wrong, she thought. It was remembering that she needed, not forgetting. Then she heard him ask the question that was swirling in her own head.

"What are you going to do with Alyssa if you move?"

"Well, I canna' take her to Scotland. She wouldna' fit in there. I've called her aunt Melinda. That's her mother's older sister. The lass needs a woman's touch. What does an old barnacle like me know about girlish things?"

"Melinda is the one who took Alyssa and little Dylan to live with her after the boat accident, isn't she?"

"Aye, that's the one. She's married to that rich geologist fella in Houston."

"Didn't they lose one of their children a few years back?"

"Aye, their little boy, Charles. Died from going into shock. Had a terrible allergic reaction to something he ate at a picnic out in the country. They couldn't get him to the hospital in time to save him. Melinda almost fell apart. Had to be treated for depression for a long time."

"It's so sad when a little child dies like that," Uncle D said softly.

"I was hopin' that raisin' Dylan and Alyssa would help pull her together and make her happy again. Melinda's not a bad sort, but nothin' like her sister, Phyllis. There'll never be another fine woman like Phyllis walkin' God's green earth. So kind and patient with her sea-lovin' husband, Robbie. God rest their souls." The old man sniffed and for a moment silence filled the air.

"Well, Mac, Alyssa wouldn't stay with them three years ago. What makes you think things will work out this time?"

Alyssa slumped back against the door frame and swallowed hard. She didn't care what her grandfather's reply would be. Right after her mother's death, Alyssa had lived with her aunt and uncle in Houston for three months. During that stay she ran away four times. It was like living in a museum. She and Dylan weren't allowed to play on the furniture or get their clothes dirty.

Alyssa hated that big, cold house with its too many rooms—especially the room that had belonged to "little Charlie." That's how her aunt always referred to the boy in the pictures that hung in every room in the house, including the bathroom. Little Charlie's bedroom was the same as it had been seven years ago when he died, and no one was allowed to go inside it. Alyssa felt sorry for her cousin Charlie. He had been her age and the few times they had played together, he was lots of fun and nicer than his younger sister, Cecile. But seeing his room and pictures was just too depressing.

And Aunt Melinda didn't allow pets like dogs or cats, and certainly not a horse. But worst of all, there was no sea at their back door. No place for Alyssa to wait and watch for her father to return. What if he walked by her at the beach one day, not knowing who or where he was? That was what had made Alyssa homesick more than anything while she stayed there.

The last time Alyssa had run away, her aunt threw up her hands in defeat and sent her niece back to Captain Mac's little shack. She couldn't understand how any child would prefer living in a filthy place like that to her own spotless home. Alyssa felt bad about leaving her brother behind. But he was barely five years old then and didn't really know what was going on.

As Alyssa listened to the old men slurping their coffee, she stared out at the ocean. The large, white-capped waves crashed ashore with a soothing rhythm. The sun was higher now, and its rays burned a spot on her arm, in spite of a few high, thin cirrus clouds. In the stiff breeze, a wind chime clacked. It was made of scallop shells Alyssa had collected on the beach and strung together with fishing line. She had painted each shell a different color of fingernail polish from old bottles that had belonged to her mother. Some kids at school had laughed at her creation as she carried it to the bus. She threw the wind chime in the trash can when she got home, but Captain Mac dug it out. He pounded a nail in a beam and strung it up. Alyssa hated to look at it, but he refused to take it down.

The sound of metal cups clanging against the

sink brought Alyssa back to the present. Then she heard the heavy scraping sound of her grandfather dragging his bad leg across the kitchen floor.

"Well, I'd better be going, Mac," Uncle D said. "I've got lots of errands in town today. The lines at the gas stations and the stores are already getting long. I gotta get some more nails so's I can finish boarding up the café. Do you reckon this one is going to hit the island?"

"My bum leg says aye, and a bad one to boot."

"Then maybe you'll need some nails, or some duct tape for the windows."

"Nay, man. I'm tired of the blasted sea and her foul temperament. I'm leavin' the place wide open this time. I'm sick of boardin' her up every time a storm blows in. And I've called that man in Freeport who said he'd buy the whole string of horses."

"Well, I sure don't envy you telling Alyssa. It's gonna break that child's heart."

"Aye. And what do ye think it's doin' to mine?"

"All right, Mac. I'll be back later today with your groceries. I'll bring you some extra bottled water and batteries, just in case."

"Thanks, Davy. You're a good man."

As the kitchen door flew open, it caught Alyssa off guard. She jumped to her feet, out of the way.

"Well, well. Now what do we have here? Where ha' ye been, lassie? Look at ye, all civered with dirt and mud like ye been wallerin' with the swine. What kind of way is that for a little lady, now?"

Captain Mac held the door open with his cane and hobbled down the steps with the help of Uncle D.

"Look at ye! *Tsch! Tsch!*" He limped into the yard, his stern blue eyes squinting under dark, craggy eyebrows that hadn't turned white like his hair. "Ye best get inside and clean up, lass. Your aunt Melinda and uncle Steven are payin' a visit this mornin'. They're bringin' your little brother and your cousin Cecile. Now, won't it be fun to have some playmates for a change?"

The thought of seeing her aunt and especially her cousin Cecile made Alyssa sick. She folded her arms and glared back at his old, sun-weathered face covered with white whiskers. His snowy hair was half hidden by a navy blue cap that he always wore, winter and summer. She wanted to tell him that she didn't need playmates, like a small child. And even her brother wasn't the same anymore since living with Aunt Melinda. He was almost like a stranger to Alyssa now. She stomped across the yard to her boat and tied it to a fence post.

"Why, look, Mac, she's brought her little green

skiff from the bay. Why do you reckon she did that?"

Captain Mac squinted at the green boat, then called to his granddaughter.

"What's ailin' ye, lass? Do ye think the hurricane's goin' to blow the wee boat across the ocean?" He laughed softly. "Sometimes I dinna ken ye a'tall. Hardly seems like three years ago this very day that Robbie took ye down to the cove and gave ye the skiff. Three long years today." He sighed heavily.

"You mean it's Alyssa's birthday?" Uncle D asked, and raised one eyebrow. "Come here, Alyssa," he called. She stepped closer and he gently patted her shoulder with his frail old hand. "Didn't know it was your birthday, sweetheart, or I'd have brought you a present." He reached into his pocket, drew out the oldest wallet in the universe, and took out a one-dollar bill. He ran it through his fingers, as if trying to remove every wrinkle, before handing it to Alyssa. She stood on her toes and planted a kiss on his Old Spice–scented face.

"Hurry now, before our company gets here," her grandfather said as he put his gnarled hand on her back. "We don't want them thinkin' I'm raisin' a savage, do we? Now skedaddle." He pushed her firmly toward the door.

Alyssa rolled her shoulder out from under his hand, then swung around to face him. She thought about what he'd said about selling the horses and sending her away. She had tried to keep her anger in, but it had been building up inside until finally she couldn't stand it another minute. She pointed to the stables and shook her head. Her lips formed the word "why," but the sound would not come out.

"What is it, lass? Is something wrong with the horses?" He stared at the stables, a confused scowl on his face.

Alyssa shook her head until her long hair flew from side to side. She wished she had her notepad with her. She pointed to the shack, the stables, to her grandfather, and then to herself, and shook her head again. The old man shrugged and sighed.

"Ah, lass, why don't ye just speak to me and tell me what's on your mind? Ye know I dinna ken what ye want." He turned to Uncle D. "Do ye understand her, Davy?"

"You know she always acts a little crazy when a big storm is coming. It's probably just some bad memories. Maybe she's worried about the horses getting hurt in the harrycane," Uncle D offered.

Captain Mac nodded thankfully. "Don't worry, Alyssa, the wee horses will be safe. Now hurry and clean up before the company gets here. Go on, ske-

daddle. You can write me a nice long note later."
He pushed her firmly toward the door again.

Alyssa heard the two old men whispering as she ran up the steps into the kitchen. The smell of coffee and bacon and biscuits left out on the Formica kitchenette filled the room, but Alyssa was too mad and frustrated to sit down and eat. She crammed a couple of pieces of bacon into her mouth and stuffed two biscuits into the front pocket of her baggy shorts.

The living room smelled like tobacco from Captain Mac's pipe. The morning light had not yet reached inside the dark room filled with old-fashioned furniture. Most of the pieces had come out of her great-grandparents' old Victorian house that had been built out of scrap lumber and bricks left over from the Great Hurricane of 1900. Captain Mac and his bride had lived there when they first got married, and so had Uncle D for most of his life. Even Alyssa's parents had stayed there when she was a baby. It was a grand, old three-story place with winding staircases and a creepy attic. Uncle D finally sold it after his wife died. Now it was a state historical site. Captain Mac had kept a few pieces of the furniture, tables and chairs covered with yellowed doilies tatted by Alyssa's grandmother.

Captain Mac could have lived in his son's

house in Pelican Village after the accident, but it was too painful for him to set foot there. So he sold that house and put the money, along with the insurance policy money, into a trust fund for Alyssa and Dylan. She wouldn't have to worry about how to pay for college. That was a great idea, she thought, but she had doubts that she would ever make it through junior high.

On her way to the cubbyhole that was her bedroom, Alyssa paused in front of a cluster of photographs on the wall next to the barometer. Everyone told her she looked like her mother because of her long blond hair and hazel eyes. But she thought she resembled her father in the photo that showed him wearing his high school baseball uniform and holding the state championship trophy. They had the same mouth and chin.

In her room, Alyssa removed a cheap lined tablet from a dark cherrywood chest of drawers. She sharpened her pencil in a plastic sharpener shaped like a miniature duck. She had won it and a little ribbon for being the best speller in the first grade. That seemed like a lifetime ago now.

Sitting on her bed cross-legged, she struggled with the words to tell her grandfather how she felt. She could make the note simple and say, "Please don't sell the horses. Please don't send me to live with Aunt Melinda again." But she felt she owed him some kind of explanation. After all, Aunt Melinda wasn't exactly mean. She never yelled or hit her. It was her attitude that irritated Alyssa—she was a perfectionist about everything. Always worried about something going to happen and always seeing the worst side of everyone. Maybe it was because of "little Charlie." Sometimes Alyssa felt sorry for her aunt and uncle, but all the same she didn't want to be around them for the rest of her life. She had enough problems of her own without having to take on the memory of a dead boy, too.

Alyssa struggled with the letter for about ten minutes, then with a grunt ripped the sheet out, wadded it up, and snapped the pencil in half.

She flopped on her back and stared out the grimy window. The only solution she could think of was to run away. But where? She sat back up and surveyed her room. There was nothing of value to take with her. She had a fantastic seashell collection she had been working on all her life and some great pieces of driftwood that she had cleaned, sanded down, and varnished. But she couldn't take those things with her. As for her clothes, all she owned were some blue jeans, T-shirts, and lots of shorts.

Alyssa crossed the room to the dark cherry-wood dresser that had belonged to her grandmother. The small, round mirror was stained everywhere except for one spot. Leaning on her elbows, she stared at her face. It was dirty all right, and her hair was still wet and tangled with clumps of sand and mud here and there. She did look awful, but she couldn't help smiling. Maybe if she looked bad enough, Aunt Melinda would throw up her hands again and refuse to take her back.

With a larger smile on her lips, she peeked out the window. The old men were still jawing out beside Uncle D's boxy-looking red Jeep Cherokee, whose chassis was raised extra high, like so many four-wheel-drive vehicles on Galveston Island.

Quickly Alyssa snuck out to the corral, bridled Stormy, then climbed on his bare back. What she needed was space in which to breathe and a little time to think before she put the words down on paper.

Stormy's muscles uncoiled like a spring as Alyssa clicked her heels on his flanks. As he charged out of the pasture and across the sandy backyard, the two men turned around.

"Come back here, lass! I told ye to get cleaned up for the company, ye little water rat." Captain Mac shook his cane in the air, but Alyssa ignored him. She leaned forward and pressed her cheek to Stormy's warm neck. She saw her grandfather's red face as the horse galloped past the Jeep.

Soon her hair was flying back as Stormy's hooves pounded on the beach. Alyssa knew at that moment what she would say in the note. She was not going to go live with her aunt and uncle and her unpleasant cousin again. If she had to, she decided, she would live on the streets or on the beach and beg for food. But no one was going to take her away from the sea and the chance that she might one day find her father.

Chapter Three

THE

MEMORY

Alyssa rode with the wind. The sea and dunes and houses flew past in a blur as Stormy's legs devoured great chunks of sandy beach.

When the gray horse began to tire, Alyssa straightened up and slowed him to a trot, then a walk. Above the tops of the dunes, she saw the bright blue tarpaulin that covered a cabin cruiser. It sat in the driveway of a geodesic dome house covered with rough cedar shingles. That was where her once best friend, Holly, lived.

There had been a time when Holly and Alyssa did everything together. They climbed trees, combed the beach for seashells, trapped crabs, built sand castles. One year they raised Easter chicks that grew up into the loudest roosters on the island. Every morning at four, Holly's father woke up cussing and throwing his shoes out the window at the roosters. He made the girls sell each one for a dollar and they got kittens to take their places.

At one time Alyssa used to ride with Holly to church. It was an old wooden building raised up on concrete blocks, and its white paint had been peeling for years. Holly's father had a deep bass voice, and when he sang the pew vibrated. Holly and Alyssa would almost die trying to hold in their giggles.

But after the charter boat accident, Holly seemed to change. She tried to pretend things were normal, but Alyssa knew Holly was uncomfortable around her. Alyssa had felt awkwardly out of place at Holly's birthday party at the roller rink. Maybe Holly hadn't intended to ignore her or whisper behind her back, but that was how it looked to Alyssa. When the skaters formed a train, Holly forgot to tell Alyssa and she sat on the sidelines feeling miserable.

Holly telephoned Alyssa twice, right after her

mother's death. But since Alyssa couldn't speak, and since Captain Mac didn't know what to say to Holly, she didn't call anymore after that.

Holly had matured faster than Alyssa, too. She already wore a bra and pantyhose and low-heeled pumps to church. At school she mostly wore skirts and colored tights. Alyssa still wore shorts or faded blue jeans and sweatshirts and ratty sneakers. And of course, Holly was now a grade ahead of Alyssa. They didn't even sit on the same pew at church anymore. Holly sat with the teenagers and flirted with boys. Alyssa sat in the last row by herself, or next to Uncle D if he attended. Then last spring, Alyssa stopped going altogether. Singing had been her favorite part of going to church, and without a voice, what was the point?

Holly had still said hello to Alyssa at school and at church until Alyssa was placed in Special Ed. That was the final stroke. After that Alyssa never saw Holly again. She missed her friend, but Alyssa didn't blame her.

After a few minutes of walking down the beach, Stormy reached the special spot where Alyssa stopped every morning. An old tree trunk lay half-buried in the sand and carved with lovers' initials. White morning glories and a pink blooming railroad vine rambled over one end. The trunk had been there since the tropical storm three years ago, its bleached limbs worn smooth like stubby amputated legs.

After dismounting Stormy, Alyssa sat on the tree trunk and stared at the dull green waters of the Gulf of Mexico. A few shrimp boats were chugging along on the horizon, and in the far distance, offshore oil drilling platforms stuck out over the water like black skeletons.

The pink-and-gold sunrise had given way to a deep blue sky. Already the air was hot and muggy. If Berta was going to hit the island, the sky at sunrise tomorrow would be blood red. The sailors' proverb that Alyssa had heard all her life about dangerous red dawns jingled in her head. It was hard to believe that a sky so apparently serene could turn into a tumultuous monster within twenty-four hours.

But even Stormy sensed that something was wrong. His nostrils flared as a sudden gust of damp wind snapped his forelock back between his pointed ears. He held his quivering gray nose in the air, breathing in the moisture and smell of salty spray. He whinnied softly, shook his mane, then began pawing a groove in the packed sand. The void promptly filled with foamy green-brown water.

For a while Alyssa passed the time watching sandpipers turn over seaweed and debris with their long, narrow beaks as they searched for food. The larger-than-usual waves had brought in many treats overnight, so the birds and ghost crabs paid little attention to the girl sitting on the tree.

The trunk felt cool and slick beneath Alyssa's legs. She couldn't help thinking about the first time she had seen the grotesque, oversized driftwood. For a long time she couldn't stand to touch its slick gray form. But later, she felt like she and the log had something in common—they both had survived the storm three years ago and they both were still on the beach waiting and watching. And both of them were hollow inside.

The tree had been the first thing Alyssa had seen when she opened her eyes after the men in yellow slickers had dragged her and the lifeboat from the ocean. They laid her on the beach beside the tree while the rest of the rescuers struggled to find her parents. Alyssa had been too tired to sit up and had felt as lifeless as the tree.

A moment later, the men in yellow laid her mother's limp body gently on the opposite side of the dead tree. They must have thought Alyssa wouldn't be able to see her mother there. But she did. Under the tree's gray belly, she saw the wedding ring on her mother's finger and the brown seaweed tangled in her legs. She watched a tall man put his hand on Captain Mac's slumped, shaking shoulders as the old man knelt over the still body.

"We're sorry, Captain Mac," a man said. "We were too late. Your daughter-in-law was pinned down and tangled up in some ropes." His voice was hoarse and deep, like that of men who haven't had their morning coffee yet.

Captain Mac's voice was quivering when he spoke.

"But my son? My Robbie?"

"We've searched everywhere, sir. His body was nowhere in the boat. One of my men thought he saw something way out, but the waves are too big. We couldn't get there. No man could survive those waves that far out. I'm sorry."

The old man's skin was as gray as the wet beard plastered to his face by the slanted rain. His sad blue eyes stared out at the roaring waves that crashed like thunder and sprayed the beach with white foam. The sound almost drowned out the wail of an approaching ambulance.

"Aye, then," he said in his thick Scottish brogue, "the sea has finally claimed her lover. I knew it would come to this one day." Captain Mac put his face in his hands as he gently sobbed. Then he lifted his head and looked at Alyssa.

"But how did the wee lass get out? What was

she doin' on Robbie's boat in a storm like this? She snuck out of my house. I didna even see she was missin' till a little while ago."

"Robbie radioed to say he was trying to help a stranded yacht. But what the child was doing on board, we don't know. There was a porthole opened up that she must have crawled through. But your son could have fit through it, too. It doesn't make sense that she got in the lifeboat and made it ashore and Robbie didn't. We'll have to ask your granddaughter what happened."

Captain Mac limped around the tree, pulled Alyssa into his shaky arms, and brushed back the hair that stuck to her face. She wanted to hug him, but she was too cold and numb and too weak to move. The rain splashed into her face, but she was too tired to even blink.

"What happened, lass?" Captain Mac asked.

It was then that Alyssa learned for the first time that she could no longer speak. She tried, but her throat felt as if the larynx were covered with crushing fingers. She wanted to cry out, but some deep sense of terror kept her tongue silent.

She told herself that she was just too exhausted to speak, that the words would come tomorrow. The next day and the next were even worse. Her lips and tongue were willing, but her brain refused to allow the words to form. Why it was happening to her, Alyssa did not understand. Three years later, and she still did not understand.

"Hey, Blondie, long time no see." A familiar voice cut into Alyssa's daydream. She glanced down the beach and saw the short guy that she had thrown into the cove only two hours ago. He held a tackle box and fishing rod in one hand and his T-shirt in the other. The wind played havoc with his shaggy, sun-streaked hair. As he walked toward Alyssa, she noticed his heavy limp.

At the tree trunk, he dropped his gear and plopped down beside Alyssa.

"Man, I'm pooped. My ankle hurts like crazy." He rubbed the swollen ankle gingerly.

Alyssa wondered if he blamed her for his hurt foot. Maybe it had happened when she shoved him into the water. She didn't know if she should feel sad or glad.

"Look," he finally said with a sigh, "I'm sorry about that green boat. I was only going to borrow it for a couple of hours so we could fish in deeper water. Ernie and Hal only came fishing with me because I told them I had a boat. I couldn't let them think it belonged to you, could I?" His pug nose crinkled up as he squinted out the morning light. "I was gonna put it back, I swear. I just got so sick of Ernie making fun of me all the time at school. Say, maybe you would let me borrow your boat sometime so we could—"

Alyssa jumped up and shook her head, making her long hair fly. Ty held up both hands and smiled.

"Okay, okay. Forget I mentioned it. Is your name Alyssa? That was the name on the boat."

She nodded.

"*Uh* . . . Hal told me you can't talk. Sorry to hear that . . . but, anyway, my name's Ty DuVal. Wanna shake hands and forget what happened this morning?"

He extended a browned, callused hand that was almost as small as Alyssa's. His grasp felt strong, but rough. She knew that he was accustomed to lots of hard work. When he grinned, his teeth looked brilliant white against his deeply tanned skin.

"Good," he said with a nod. "Well, I've got a long walk ahead of me. That stupid Ernie and Hal took their bikes and wouldn't give me a lift. Then I sprained my ankle chasing them. They wouldn't even come back for me. They're still mad about the boat and for getting all wet." He talked as he slid the Batman T-shirt over his head and compact, muscular shoulders. As he rose to his feet, he grimaced.

Alyssa wasn't sure why she felt sorry for him, but she did know what it felt like to be rejected by your friends. She pointed to his ankle and patted Stormy's back. Then she waved her arm as if to say go on up. Ty understood her right away.

"You're crazy, girl. That's too dangerous. I might fall off of ol' Trigger there. Where's the saddle? Besides, I'm too short anyhow." He rambled off a dozen excuses and began limping down the beach. Alyssa slowly led Stormy behind the boy until he stopped.

Alyssa laughed to herself at his cowardly behavior, but she kept her face serious. After pointing to Stormy's back and his sprained ankle one more time, she formed a cup with her hands.

"You are a stubborn one, ain't you?" Ty shook his head and protested again, but finally he put his unsprained foot in her hands. Alyssa lifted him up, kept him from sliding over the other side, then grabbed a hank of mane and pulled herself up in front of Ty.

They hadn't gone very far when she saw Ty's tackle box and fishing rod lying near the tree trunk where he had dropped them earlier. She helped him dismount and watched him pick up the items.

"Thanks, Blondie. I forgot all about my fishing gear." He looked at the rod and reel in his hands a minute, then sighed. "Man, I feel like a fool going home without any fish. I told Ernie and Hal that I didn't need them. Now look at me—no fish and a banged-up foot. Man, I'm a jerk." He picked up a scallop shell and tossed it far out into the ocean. A sea gull dived at it, then screamed in protest.

Alyssa bit her lip, trying to think of what she could do to let him know that she understood how he felt. Suddenly she thought of something. She tapped his shoulder, then pointed toward the cove.

"What's wrong?" he asked.

Alyssa held her hands about fifteen inches apart, then pointed toward the inland side of the island again. Ty's vivid blue eyes looked blank as he studied her hands. He shrugged.

"I don't get it," he said.

Alyssa wanted to scream. Pointing toward the ocean and pretending to reel in a fishing rod didn't work, either. She was almost ready to give up when Ty picked up a long stick and handed it to her.

"Write it in the sand."

Alyssa leaned over and quickly drew the outline of a fish on the beach.

"Are you talking about fish?" Ty asked with a laugh.

Alyssa nodded so hard that her hair fell into her eyes. Then she held her hands fifteen inches apart again.

"Wow! That big! Let's go!" This time Ty had no trouble getting up on Stormy's back.

As they rode along toward the leeward side of the island, Ty patted her shoulder affectionately.

"You know, Blondie, I'm glad I met you today. You're really nice. It'll be more fun fishing with you than with Ernie and Hal."

Alyssa felt herself blushing. She couldn't remember the last time someone had called her "nice." It had probably been her mother. She didn't know if Ty really meant it, but she hoped that he wouldn't end up being mad and frustrated with her, like everyone else. But maybe that was asking too much.

T Y

It wasn't a bad day, considering that there was a hurricane in the Gulf. Clouds had crept into the sky over the horizon, high wispy streaks that looked like pulled-apart cotton candy. Occasionally a pickup or a van loaded with plywood would stop at a beach house, where owners were busily boarding up windows. And of course there were the crazy ones who came to the beach just for the giant waves. Surfers, some in wet suits, took their boards or air mattresses out and let the combers roll them in.

Soon Alyssa and Ty had crossed Termini Road and were traveling back to the inward side of the island, leaving behind the houses and people. Cows grazed lazily in pastures, unaware of what might lie in store for them in the next day or so. At their hooves, white egrets picked for insects.

When they reached the cove, Alyssa tethered Stormy to a tallow sapling and found a clear area of water. She had fished there many times with her father and usually had good luck. Especially when a storm was approaching.

Ty opened his small orange tackle box. It was the cheap kind sold at discount stores. He lifted out a smelly plastic bag.

"Here's some bait," he said. "If there's one thing I've got plenty of, it's shrimp. My stepdaddy owns a shrimp boat."

Alyssa helped Ty untangle his fishing line, then slipped a hook into a small shrimp.

"Wanna hear something funny?" he finally said. "I was supposed to stay home today and help my stepdaddy repair nets." With a flick of his wrist, Ty cast out the line, making the reel sing as it unwound. The sinker hit the water with a plop, and little ripples circled out across the cove. "Man, I hate repairing nets. Makes me sick."

Ty handed Alyssa the rod, placing it in her hands very gently, as if she didn't know how to handle it.

"You hold it a while," he said. "You've probably got better luck than me. I'm about the unluckiest guy in the world."

Alyssa peered into his face as he settled down, wondering why he had said that. He started talking, only half paying attention to the fishing. His family rented a little house right on the bay. During the summer, Ty spent most of his time on the shrimp boat helping his stepfather, Randon. Once in a while his mother and younger sisters helped out on weekends. Ty was the header, the person who had to break the heads off the shrimp. It was about the worst job on the boat, and he hated it.

All the time Alyssa listened, her fingers worked on the reel, slowly drawing the line in and recasting if she didn't feel a nibble. Suddenly she felt a tug move up the line, then another stronger one. She flicked the rod to set the hook and heard the whine as the fish took off.

"Hey, you've got something!" Ty said, leaping up. "Hurry, reel it in."

Alyssa reeled and tugged, pulling the fish closer.

"I sure hope it's a flounder," Ty said. "My stepdaddy loves flounder. Maybe if I bring one home, he won't be so mad about my sprained ankle."

The fish broke out of the water.

"It's a big one!" Ty shouted as he leaned over and scooped the fighting fish into his short-handled net. Alyssa saw the pinkish tint and the dark spot near its tail.

"A redfish," Ty said as he unhooked it. He slipped the stringer wire through the gills, then plopped the fish back into the cove. He staked the stringer rope in the ground. "Nice going, Blondie. Now just catch me a flounder."

Alyssa nodded and motioned for Ty to follow her down the shore. It was midmorning and already hot, so she figured the flounder would be hiding under the sandy silt where it was a little cooler. At night and during the cool parts of the day, they would be closer to the grasses, waiting for food. It wasn't time for their autumn run yet. Around October or November the flounder were so plentiful, sometimes Alyssa would step on one accidentally. That was the time when they migrated from the shallow bay into the deep Gulf of Mexico to spawn in warmer waters. They would stay there all winter and come back, along with their young, during the spring. You could catch some during the summer if you knew where to look. It wasn't easy, but finding one was a true test of fishing skill. And the struggle was worth it—a flounder was great eating.

Ty and Alyssa walked toward a spot that was shaded by some tall reeds. Alyssa turned the shrimp bait over in her hands, a frown on her face. Flounders preferred live bait, especially mud minnows and finger mullet. If they had brought along a seine, they could have caught some minnows. But she had no choice except to use the dead shrimp. She hooked one, then cast out toward the shady spot and slowly pulled in the line. Nothing moved, so she cast again, this time slightly to the right of where she'd cast before. Slowly she reeled the line in again.

Ty stared at her in amazement as if he'd never seen anyone fish before. Alyssa wished she could talk so she could tell Ty all she knew about flounder fishing, how they buried themselves in the shallow water in beds of sand or mud and blended in so well that only their socketed eyes protruded. There they waited patiently for food to swim by them. Uncle D called it "eating in bed," because the flounder waits for its meal to come to it instead of swimming around looking for food. That also makes the fish easy to gig with a spear since they don't move until the fisherman is right on top of them.

"You're pretty smart for a girl," Ty finally said, patting her back. "Most girls I know don't like to fish or get their feet muddy. Who taught you to fish and to ride that horse? Your daddy?"

Alyssa felt her face turn hot and quickly turned her head away. Her throat got tight and she had to swallow again and again. When she glanced back at Ty, he was studying her carefully. She nodded.

"Well, your dad must be derned smart. My daddy taught me everything, too. In Louisiana. We were shrimpers there, in a town so little you could spit from one end to the other. Things were a lot different when he was alive. We lived in a nice house, and I didn't have to help out on the boat at all. My dad was the smartest shrimper in the whole town. Everybody said so. He wanted me to go to college and do something different, though, when I grew up."

Ty's fingers toyed with the shrimp bait as he stared across the bay.

"I was just a little kid, but I remember him a lot. He's dead now."

Alyssa drew in a sharp breath and tapped Ty's arm.

"What is it?" he asked.

She pointed at her chest, then nodded. But Ty screwed up his face and shook his head.

"I don't get it, Blondie. Can you write it down?"

She broke off a reed and scribbled in the damp sand. "My dad gone, too."

"Oh, I'm sorry. You mean he died, like mine?"

Alyssa shook her head as hard as she could. She quickly wrote in the sand: "Gone."

Ty's face remained blank a moment, then he shrugged. "Sorry. Do you have a stepfather?"

Alyssa shook her head.

"Well, you're lucky. My mom had to remarry. She had too many kids and lots of bills to pay. The government authorities were going to split us up and put us in foster homes, so she married Randon. Sometimes I think she regrets it. Anyway, we moved to Texas last year and he bought a shrimp boat. Randon didn't used to be so bad, but since he got that boat, he's been drinking more and getting meaner. He's got too many bills to pay and . . . ah, forget it. Hey, you've got another bite!"

Alyssa felt the tug on the line. It could have been a crab, or a snag, or a flounder. Slowly she counted to five. Flounders hold their food between sharp teeth for several seconds before eating it. If a fisherman strikes his line too fast, he simply jerks it from the flounder's mouth and ends up with nothing. Alyssa felt the line moving and knew it was a flounder. She began reeling in and saw the shadowy fish quickly scoot away about ten feet then bury itself into the sand again. It grew perfectly quiet.

Ty laughed. "He thinks he's safe hidden there. Here, let me bring him in. Come on, little fishy, come to Papa," he said as he took the rod from Alyssa's hand.

Alyssa watched his face light up for the next few minutes while he reeled in the peculiar-looking flat fish. When it was close enough, she scooped the shining flounder into Ty's net. The fish weighed about two and a half pounds, a perfect meal for one hungry person. Its eyes, both on the same side of its head, moved in different directions on stalks. Already the changeable skin on its front side had turned from speckled brown to dark gray and now contrasted sharply with its pearly white bottom side.

As Ty started to remove the hook with his finger, Alyssa yanked his hand back. She shook her head and pointed to two sharp teeth glistening inside its mouth.

"Oh, thanks," Ty said. "I've got some needle-nosed pliers inside my tackle box somewhere."

Alyssa dug around for the tool, then watched the slippery fish fight until the hook was out. She carefully slipped the stringer wire though its lips and gently placed it back into the bay.

"We're gonna eat good tonight," Ty said cheerfully as he rebaited another hook. But the flounder eluded them for the next hour. All they caught were more redfish and two small ocean trout.

Ty didn't talk about his stepfather anymore. He laughed and joked and acted frustrated because he couldn't catch a flounder. Alyssa found herself grinning like a fool most of the time. Finally they used up all the bait. Ty insisted that Alyssa was his lucky charm, but she knew that the fish had come in with the approaching storm.

After reeling in the last fish, Ty stood and stretched his muscular arms. "I sure am hungry. Wish I could eat that flounder right now. Don't you?"

Alyssa jumped up and quickly piled some leaves and dry sticks into a cleared spot and started a fire with the miniature cigarette lighter that she always carried in her pocket. Ty's eyes opened wide as he watched her crouch over the little bundle of kindling. Then she removed a pocketknife from her other pocket and handed it to Ty.

"*Hmm* . . . I guess this means I'm supposed

to clean the fish, right? Okay, I guess that's fair since you started the fire. But if you don't mind, I'd like to save the flounder for my stepdaddy; it's his favorite. Let's eat one of these trout for now, okay?"

Alyssa agreed. By the time he had scraped and gutted the fish, the fire was blazing and the sweet aroma of burning wood filled the air. Carefully she worked the two fish halves onto a sharpened stick and held it over the flame. Quickly the pieces curled and turned dark. Alyssa produced the two biscuits she'd placed in her pocket early that morning.

Ty chuckled and stuck his hand inside her back pocket. He jerked out the slingshot.

"What else do you have in your pockets, a bicycle?"

Alyssa slapped his hand. She made two small sandwiches out of the biscuits and fish. Ty devoured his like a starving pig.

"*Mmm* . . . So you're not only pretty, but you can cook, too."

Alyssa felt her face flush. No one had called her pretty since her mother had been alive.

After finishing the fish, they smothered the fire and stretched out on a patch of cool grass under an old cottonwood tree a few yards away. The wind swishing through the canes and rubbing the stalks together and the clacking cottonwood leaves sounded like music to Alyssa. Sleepiness crept over her and she closed her eyes.

"You know," Ty said, waking Alyssa out of a doze, "you're not like the other girls at school. And it's not just because you can't talk. You listen to me, I mean really listen. And you don't act like I'm some kind of trash because I work on a shrimp boat most of the time. Sometimes the guys call me names . . . ah, forget it." Ty rolled over onto his stomach. He drew little figures in a spot of dirt for a long time before looking up again. His dirty blond hair flopped down over one blue eye.

"Do you know I'm the shortest guy in the eighth grade?" he asked as he sat up and faced Alyssa. "How old do you think I am?"

She held up her fingers until they added up to thirteen, her own age.

Ty hissed between his teeth, then smacked the dirt with his hand. "See! Everybody thinks I'm a kid. It's Momma's fault. I was real sick when I was seven, and she made me repeat the first grade and the second grade, too. She makes me so mad sometimes, that woman. I'm really fifteen." He snapped a stick in two and tossed it into the bayou, then spat at it.

"I lie about my age most of the time and tell everybody I'm fourteen. I don't want them thinking I'm a dummy. You know, you're the first person I've ever told my real age to." He turned to face Alyssa. "Now, promise me you won't go telling the kids at school, okay?"

She held a finger to her chest and crossed her heart. Ty patted her shoulder fondly.

"You're a good kid, Blondie, no matter what Hal says. Well, I'd better be getting home. It's gonna take me a long time to get there with this bum foot."

Alyssa glanced down at his ankle. It was swollen twice its normal size and looked blue in one spot. She remembered what her father had done for her sprained ankle once. She motioned for Ty to sit down, then tied his T-shirt as tightly as possible around the ankle. She helped him to his feet and brought Stormy over.

"Thanks," he said. "Just take me as far as the main road. I'll hitch a ride home from there. I do it all the time when my bike's busted, like it is now. I know people. They'll feel sorry for a cute little short boy by the side of the road with a sore foot and a stringer of fish." He grinned and winked.

After retrieving the stringer from the cove, Alyssa helped Ty mount Stormy. When they reached Termini Road, they slid to the ground and he shook her hand.

"Thanks, Blondie. It's been nice meeting you."

Alyssa nodded. She wanted so much to say something and wished that she had brought her notepad and pencil. But she had left her grandfather's shack in a hurry. She wanted to tell Ty that he wasn't like the other boys at school. He was nice. He "listened" to her, too, even though she wasn't talking. For the first time in three years, she felt as if she had carried on an actual conversation with someone. She wanted to tell him she liked him, even though he had tried to steal her green boat. She wanted to tell him she hoped his foot would get better and that Ernie and Hal got showed up by all the fish he'd caught that day. She wanted, wanted, wanted.

The words almost came to her lips. Her mind had been so concentrated on Ty that, for just a brief instant, a fraction of a word spilled out.

"I . . ."

Ty's eyebrows shot up.

"Yes? Go ahead," he said calmly, placing a tanned hand on her shoulder. It felt hot and rough.

Alyssa swallowed hard. Like a sleeping guard who awakens to see a prisoner trying to climb over the compound wall, her mind panicked. Her heart thumped against her rib cage, and once again the steel fingers gripped her throat and stifled the rest of her sentence.

"Do you want to say something?" Ty asked, coaxing her with a smile. "I can wait a little while for you." He shifted his weight from the hurt foot.

By now Alyssa's breath was coming in short gasps, and the feeling of dread and near nausea was rolling through her stomach. She quickly shook her head and backed away. The confused look on Ty's face pained Alyssa, so she forced a smile and shrugged. Then she put her hand to her forehead and saluted, like she'd seen John Wayne do in the old westerns when he was leaving someone he admired. The instant after she had done it, she felt stupid.

But Ty returned the salute. After studying Alyssa's face a long time, he shook his head. "Bye, Blondie. See you again sometime." With that, he limped away.

Alyssa watched his back and his hard calf muscles tightening with each step. She felt a lump rise in her throat and a misty layer form on her eyes. She blinked to bring Ty into focus.

Suddenly he stopped, swung around, and walked back toward her.

"Here, you take the flounder," he said as he removed the fish from the stringer. He slid a piece of twine through its gills and tied a knot. "You deserve this more than I do."

Alyssa shook her head in protest and pushed

the flat fish back toward him. She didn't want to take his prize.

"Come on, stubborn. If you take it, I promise to come back tomorrow morning. We can catch some more flounder. Meet me at the same cove about seven o'clock. Okay?"

Alyssa didn't want to take his flounder. She knew he wanted to impress his stepfather with it. Her heart ached with admiration for his generosity. But she didn't want to hurt his feelings, either, so she took the fish. Besides, she decided, if they met at the cove tomorrow she would come prepared for floundering. She would bring a seine to catch some live mud minnows. And she'd bring her green skiff and wading boots and a gig. She'd catch a dozen flounder for him. She smiled and nodded.

"Great!" Ty gave the thumbs-up signal and grinned. "See you in the morning."

Ty didn't turn around again as he walked to the side of the road. He stuck his thumb out expertly. A small Jeep loaded with teenagers crunched to a halt, and he crawled into the back seat. Laughter and squeals filled the air as he tossed the stringer of fish onto the floorboard. Alyssa felt a stab of jealousy when she heard Ty talking and laughing with the girls. She watched the Jeep and its noisy passengers rumble out of sight.

As she rode Stormy toward her grandfather's stables, Alyssa thought about the fish she was carrying. Captain Mac loved flounder, too. He was the best cook she knew, and they hadn't eaten flounder in a long time. When he saw the fish, he'd probably slap her back and shake with laughter. She felt good and couldn't wait to show it to him.

As she arrived at the stables, she saw an unfamiliar car in the driveway. It was a silver Mercedes-Benz with a personalized license plate that said Wilson. A shiver raced through her body. Her aunt and uncle's last name was Wilson.

Then she saw her cousin Cecile dressed in the most ridiculous outfit for a day at the beach, something all white and frilly. Alyssa recalled everything her grandfather had said that morning about sending her away and selling the horses.

Suddenly Alyssa's good feeling vanished.

D Y L A N

No one saw Alyssa as she moved Stormy onto a grass-covered dune and looked down at Captain Mac's yard. Although they were her own kin, the people below didn't seem real to her. She should have been glad to see them, especially her brother, Dylan. The last time Alyssa had seen him was the Christmas before, but he had been sick and didn't get to play. She guessed she loved him. She wanted to, but each time she saw him he seemed less and less like the little boy she had known and helped raise. That little kid had laughed a lot and was constantly crawling into trouble and had been tanned from playing on the beach. The boy below was skinny and pale. He was wearing dark-rimmed glasses and didn't seem interested in the ocean at all, or anything else around him. He hid behind Aunt Melinda like a timid mouse.

Aunt Melinda wore a white pleated skirt and a brightly flowered blouse that emphasized her light complexion and dark hair. Alyssa could hardly believe that Melinda was her mother's older sister. Her mom had had blond hair and strong, tanned arms and legs from working on the charter boat and in her gardens all summer long. Aunt Melinda's soft face was already starting to get sunburned. She constantly wiped her sweaty brow with a limp tissue.

Cecile was two years younger than Alyssa but acted older. Her black, curly hair bounced as she pranced to the horse corral. Her frilly outfit looked like a dress, but Alyssa couldn't believe that a kid would wear something that impractical to the beach. Most beach-goers quickly learned that white clothes usually ended up with hunks of black tar balls stuck on them.

Alyssa liked her uncle Steven's looks, even if he didn't have much hair on top of his head. What was left was dark and curly like Cecile's. He was rich, but he wasn't stuck up about having a lot of money. He was a geologist for an oil company in Houston. His terrific rock collection was probably the only thing about living with the family that had interested Alyssa. Uncle Steven had taught her the names of different rocks and gems and had bought her a little tumbler to polish pieces of agate they found on a country road. Then one day Cecile played with the tumbler and ruined it. After Alyssa had rolled Cecile on the ground and sat on her chest, Aunt Melinda took Cecile's side. That was what prompted Alyssa to run away for good and never go back.

Alyssa knew she could have turned Stormy around and returned to the cove to wait until everyone left. But in a way she wanted to get the meeting over with once and for all. She wanted to make it perfectly clear to Captain Mac that she was *not* going to live with her aunt and uncle again.

After taking a deep breath, Alyssa nudged Stormy down the dune. The people in the yard stared at her. Her grandfather's squinting eyes crucified her from under the shaggy eyebrows that looked like bird nests. Alyssa put Stormy in the corral and slowly approached the house, holding the flounder out from her body like a peace offering.

She could hardly see Dylan because he had scooted behind Aunt Melinda's skirt. It seemed to Alyssa that her little brother had grown a foot since the last time she had seen him, and his hair was darker than she remembered. At first she thought he was sucking his thumb, even though he was eight years old. Then she realized he was biting his fingernails.

Alyssa was shocked to see how much Dylan looked like their father—the brown hair, brown eyes, and a dent in his chin. Except for the glasses and the pale face, he looked exactly like an old photo of their father that hung on a wall in Captain Mac's living room.

Alyssa knew that she was dirty from being knocked into the cove earlier that morning and from sitting on a sandy bank and wading in the flats. But she didn't expect what happened next.

Cecile started giggling and pointing at the flounder. She held her turned-up, piggish nose and made faces as if the fish stank. Alyssa's cheeks turned hot. The flounder had only stopped kicking a few minutes before and was far from being spoiled. Then Dylan joined in. He not only held his nose, he also backed up and gasped for air as if the fish were poisoned gas. Then his face turned a deep shade of red as he broke into a fit of coughing.

"Aunt Melinda—a fish!" he screamed between coughs. "I'm going to die!"

"Oh no," Aunt Melinda said, drawing Dylan close to her side and stepping several feet back. An expression of panic spread across her face and her eyes had a look that reminded Alyssa of a cornered wild animal. "Take that smelly old fish away," she cried in a strained voice. "Dylan is allergic to fish. Steven . . . should we go to the doctor?"

"Now, Melinda, it's all right," Uncle Steven said in a calm, reassuring voice. "Remember what the doctor said. Dylan's not allergic to fish."

"I don't care what the doctor said," Melinda shouted. "They didn't know little Charlie was allergic to anything, did they? I *know* what an allergic reaction looks like." She pulled Dylan even farther away and told him to stay there. By now Dylan had stopped coughing, and his fingers were stuck in his mouth again.

Confusion clouded Alyssa's face. She did not understand what her aunt was saying. Dylan hadn't been allergic to fish three years ago. He had eaten a lot of fish when he was younger. He had loved any kind of seafood.

Alyssa turned to her grandfather for support. Surely he would realize Aunt Melinda was wrong. Not only about Dylan but about the fish. It wasn't a smelly old thing. It was a flounder, his favorite. She held it out for him.

"Ah, lass," Captain Mac said as he thumped his cane on the packed sand. "What have ye gotten into this time? Ye're even dirtier than ye were this mornin'." He shook his head as he turned to Melinda. "I told her to get cleaned up for company, but she skedaddled out and went fishin'. The child loves to fish, just like my Robbie, and I'll not hold that against her." He chuckled lightly.

"But, Captain MacAllister, she's filthy. No girl, even one who has been fishing, should go around looking like that. She looks like a street urchin. And her hair is tangled and muddy. It's disgraceful."

Alyssa hated to hear people talk about her as if she couldn't hear them. She would have screamed if she could. She glanced at her uncle, who stood by quietly listening. While the others were arguing, he leaned closer to Alyssa and touched the fish.

"It's a flounder, isn't it?" he whispered.

Alyssa nodded.

"Do you know how to cook it?"

Alyssa hesitated. She could cook fish, but there was something that her grandfather did—the spices he always used—that made his flounder taste better. She wasn't sure if she should answer yes or no, so she shrugged.

"Well, maybe Captain Mac will bake it for us.

I haven't eaten flounder in over a year." He winked and placed his hand on Alyssa's shoulder, steering her closer to her brother. "Look at the fish, Dylan. It's a flounder. Want to touch it? Come on, it won't bite." Steven pushed Alyssa a little closer to the pale-faced boy with the eyes of a scared and lost dog. Dylan backed up, shaking his head.

"It'll make me sick," Dylan said, then stuck his fingers back in his mouth and chewed on his nails again. "It'll make me die."

Uncle Steven sighed. "You're not going to die, Dylan. The doctors said you're not allergic to fish or anything else. How'd you like to go fishing today? We can buy some bait and rent some tackle and go down to the jetties. There should be some great fish out there today. What do you say, Dylan?" he softly urged the boy to come closer.

Alyssa's brother shook his head and scooted away. He glanced at Aunt Melinda, who was still busily talking to Captain Mac and not paying attention to the boy.

Uncle Steven sighed heavily and slumped his shoulders. Slowly he straightened up to his full height, which was a bit taller than Alyssa's own father had been. A sad expression clouded his face.

On impulse Alyssa decided to help her uncle. She stepped closer to Dylan, holding the limp, beady-eyed fish near the boy's face. She wanted him to touch it and learn that it wouldn't hurt him. But Dylan let out a scream, and his face turned red again. He doubled over, shrieking until big tears rolled down his cheeks. Alyssa couldn't believe that this was her own brother. What had her aunt done to him?

Aunt Melinda stopped in midsentence, swirled around, and gasped.

"What happened?" she demanded, as she rushed to Dylan and leaned down to his level. She wiped his tears with a tissue.

"Alyssa stuck that dead fish in his face," Cecile said.

Alyssa knew Cecile had not been watching them. She had been pulling yellow buttercups and pink goatshead morning glories that grew along the fence rails near the corral a few yards away.

"Why did you do that, Alyssa?" Aunt Melinda asked in a strained voice. Alyssa thought the woman wanted to knock her across the yard. Her eyes flashed with anger. "I told you Dylan is allergic to fish. He has developed terrible allergies over the past three years since he's been living with us. He can't be around anything dirty."

Alyssa wanted to tell her aunt that the fish wasn't dirty. How could something that has spent its life in water be unclean? She opened her mouth and moved her tongue. As usual, the sound got no farther than her throat before the panic gripped her chest.

All eyes turned on Alyssa. She glanced at Captain Mac, wishing he would speak up for her. Why didn't he tell Aunt Melinda to leave her alone? Why didn't he tell her that flounder was a great delicacy and that catching one at this time of year took a special skill?

But instead of speaking in her defense, Captain Mac just leaned on his cane with one hand and rubbed his nose with the other as if he didn't care. Alyssa wished the old man could see that Aunt Melinda was turning his grandson into a soft-shelled shrimp. Her brother was Dylan, god of the ocean, son of the waves. He should have been fishing and swimming and running wild along the beaches. He should have been playing in the sand and dirt and waves, not coughing and wheezing at everything.

Alyssa decided her grandfather was not going to help her. He obviously did not want to get involved in this argument. Then Cecile giggled again. Alyssa felt heat flood over her face, even though there was a strong ocean breeze. She was mad at Dylan for being such a baby, and mad at Cecile for being so spiteful, and mad at her grandfather for saying nothing.

"You mustn't tease poor little Dylan," Aunt Melinda said in a preachy voice as she patted Dylan's skinny back. "He's a sick little boy. We have to treat him very special. Now, throw that old fish back into the ocean. We want to go to a nice restaurant today. After all, it's your birthday." She forced a smile.

Alyssa turned to her grandfather one last time for help. She held the flounder up toward him, pleading with her eyes. How could the old man forget all the times he had talked about the autumn flounder run? He always looked forward to it and to cooking his favorite fish. But the stern eyes didn't flinch.

"Do as your auntie asks, lass. Ye can always catch another fish later."

Suddenly Alyssa remembered how badly Ty had wanted the flounder. He had been so proud of it and wanted to give it to his stepdaddy to avoid getting into trouble. But he had given it to Alyssa instead as a token of his friendship. And now these relatives were asking her to throw it away as if it were a piece of bilge-water trash.

Alyssa opened her mouth and tried to force a word out. But the only sound she made was a grunt and a squeak. Hot tears filled her eyes. Everyone stared at her, but it was Cecile's smug face that grated on her nerves the most.

With a grunt, Alyssa swung the string with the flounder on it, then let go. It hit Cecile broadside on the front of her new white dress, then slid onto her new white sandals.

Cecile screamed and jumped back, then began crying. After a few seconds, Dylan joined in as if he didn't want Cecile to get all the attention.

"Alyssa!" Captain Mac shouted. But she was already stomping toward the house. "Come back here and apologize, ye little heathen!"

Maybe she was a heathen, and not civilized and fancy, Alyssa thought as she bounded up the concrete steps. But at least when she got mad, she didn't act like everything was okay and force a smile even though she wanted to punch someone in the nose. That was the same thing as lying, wasn't it? Didn't the preacher always tell them to be honest? Well, she was being honest and trying to tell her family the truth: she would rather be an orphan than live with her aunt Melinda and Cecile in a big city away from the ocean.

Chapter Six

BEFORE

THE

STORM

The screen door slammed shut behind Alyssa as she plunged into her grandfather's shack. At the kitchen sink she stopped to wash her face and looked through the grimy window at the people in the yard. She imagined they were saying how horrible she was, how dirty and uncivilized. They were right, she thought, as she looked down at her broken fingernails and muddy sneakers.

With a sigh of frustration, she crossed the dimly lit living room, pausing in front of a mahogany table littered with framed photographs. She chose one of her favorites and carried it to her bedroom. After removing her shoes, she flopped onto her back and studied the picture.

The photo had been taken the day her father had bought his charter boat and christened it. Her mother was smiling, but Alyssa remembered that her mom had been worried. Her father had quit his city job to start his own business. But in spite of her misgivings, Alyssa's mom assured her daughter that everything would be all right. She was going to return to teaching full-time when the new school year started.

Alyssa was standing on a piling between her parents, so that her face was almost even with her mother's. Dylan was still in diapers in his mother's arms. A sea gull was flying overhead, almost dead center in the photograph. When her father saw the bird in the picture, he laughed and said it was Sammy Sea Gull trying to become a famous star like Jonathan Livingston Seagull. Alyssa's father called all sea gulls that acted bold and came close "Sammy." There was one bird that would bravely eat out of Alyssa's hand when she stood on top of the boat and held up a piece of bread.

Alyssa stared at the skinny little girl in the picture. She didn't remember being so young. Her father had let her try to bust the champagne bottle across the charter boat's prow. She couldn't do it, so her mother tried. She struck it with a powerful blow and the bottle exploded, spraying pink fizz all over them. Alyssa's father named the boat *Bonnie Lass* because that was what Captain Mac called her and her mother.

Just thinking about those days sometimes made Alyssa relax. And she was tired because she had tossed and turned the night before. She wanted to fall asleep to escape the people outside, but suddenly the screen door banged and she heard people talking in the kitchen. Then she heard footsteps stop at her bedroom door. Alyssa closed her eyes and pretended to be asleep.

"You have to take the lass with a wee bit o' salt, Melinda. Losin' both parents is something that would turn any child sour."

"I realize that, Captain Mac, but I didn't know she'd gotten so bad. The last time we saw her she was quiet and withdrawn, but not so violent. There's no telling what she might do to the other children. I hope you understand my position. I'm just not sure . . ."

"Melinda," Uncle Steven's voice broke in, "we promised to at least give it a try."

"Well, I think she really can talk but is refusing on purpose to get attention," Aunt Melinda said. "Captain Mac, we spoke to a child psychiatrist about her last week and he agreed to examine her. He thinks hypnosis may work. You know we're willing to help. She *is* my only niece. But we can do just so much. She has to cooperate."

"I told you the episode with the fish was my fault," Uncle Steven interrupted. He sounded annoyed. "I was trying to make Dylan look at it and Alyssa just wanted to help. Now, why don't we go eat lunch. Let's try that new restaurant on Seawall Boulevard. I'm starving and we've still got more boarding up to do before the hurricane hits."

Even from her bed, Alyssa heard her aunt sigh.

"Oh, all right, I suppose you're right," she said. She tiptoed across the squeaky plank floor.

"Alyssa," she whispered, gently shaking her niece's arm. "Wake up."

Alyssa stared into her aunt's eyes. They were the same color as her mother's had been, but the short, dark hair touched with premature gray looked nothing like her mother's long, flowing blond hair.

"We're going to a restaurant for lunch, Alyssa. Why don't you take a bath and change into some nice clothes." She paused a minute, then spoke faster. "I'm sorry I yelled at you about that fish. Let's just pretend it never happened, okay?"

Alyssa shrugged and pushed off the bed. After a quick shower, she broke her cheap plastic comb trying to get a knot out of her hair. She finally gave up and pulled her hair back into a ponytail, tangles and all.

Back in her room, Alyssa stood in front of her closet staring at three skirt-and-blouse sets hanging on a warped clothes pole. Her mother had bought them the day before she'd been killed. They had planned to go shopping again the very next day. Many times Alyssa thought that if only they had gone shopping as planned, her mother would still be alive.

Alyssa didn't remember growing, yet when she tried on the skirts, they were too tight and she couldn't reach the buttons on the back of one of the blouses. In the far corner of the closet she saw a dress that had been too big three years ago. Her mother had been waiting for her to grow into it. Alyssa slipped it over her head and found that it fit very well. But it was an Easter dress, covered with a layer of dotted Swiss. It was stiff and itchy, and she couldn't tie a straight bow in the back. When Alyssa stepped into the living room, Aunt Melinda sucked in her breath and Cecile broke into giggles.

"Well," Aunt Melinda said, and cleared her throat. "It certainly is an interesting dress, Alyssa. But I think it's a little too fancy for the restaurant."

"Mommy, she's wearing sneakers," Cecile whispered.

"Alyssa, dear, don't you think a skirt and blouse would be nice? That's what Cecile is going to wear, isn't it, angel?"

Cecile nodded. "My blue Missy Christy split skirt and suspenders and the white blouse with the bluebird embroidered on the pocket. We bought them at Neiman's last week, remember? They're out in the car."

Aunt Melinda nodded. "I remember, angel. Now, Alyssa, I think this dress is too frilly. Why don't you save it for church? Where are your new school clothes?"

Alyssa tried not to heave a sigh. She didn't have any new school clothes. She didn't want any, either. She liked wearing old blue jeans and comfortable T-shirts, in case she needed to run fast or got in a fight with one of the boys who were always teasing her. Like that boy Hal.

Alyssa thought about writing all this down on a notepad but decided that Aunt Melinda wouldn't understand. She would probably just get all huffy and mad and tell her niece not to fight boys. So Alyssa crossed the room, jerked the closet door open, and stepped aside to let Aunt Melinda see for herself.

Cecile and her mother stuck their noses inside the closet. The room filled with squeaky noises as the two shoved clothes from one end of the pole to the other. Cecile started to giggle again, but Aunt Melinda told her to hush and forced another smile.

"Well . . ." Aunt Melinda drew in a deep breath. "I've got an idea. Why don't we dash over to Galvez Mall before we eat to pick up a few school clothes for you, Alyssa. Would that be all right?"

Cecile's eyes lit up.

"Oh, Mommy, let's do it. I need some new clothes, too."

"But, angel, we've been shopping for your school clothes all month. Don't you have enough? Daddy's already complaining about the charge account bills."

"But I need a new belt. And I forgot to bring any extra shoes. I want to change before we go to the restaurant."

Alyssa felt nauseous at the thought of shopping with her aunt and cousin. Shopping had been fun with her mother. But for the past three years, her grandfather just gave her money for clothes twice a year, spring and fall, and let her pick out what she wanted. Sometimes he looked disappointed to see what she bought, but he had only recently been lecturing her on dressing more ladylike.

Suddenly Alyssa felt like a prisoner. She knew they would end up shopping no matter how much she protested. She shrugged as if she didn't care, knowing that she would never wear whatever they chose, especially if it resembled anything that Cecile wore.

Uncle Steven drove to his beach house first so Cecile could change out of her fishy-smelling clothes. Alyssa didn't bother to get out of the car. She had been inside before and knew what it looked like—all white and clean, with machines that filtered dust from the air. Most of the year her aunt and uncle rented it out to vacationers, but at the moment it was empty. Fresh sheets of yellow pine plywood were stacked up in the carport.

Shopping at the mall was even worse than Alyssa had imagined. Cecile rummaged through clothes, tossing them aside for being the wrong color or style and complained that there weren't enough fancy department stores. She turned up her nose at things that almost any girl would like. Aunt Melinda selected a frilly, blue jumpsuit with pale flowers for Alyssa and a training bra that itched and squeezed her until she felt like she had a bad case of heartburn. After slipping into the jumpsuit, Alyssa stared at herself in the mirror. She looked stupid, she thought, no doubt about it. The clothes fit her well, but she didn't fit the clothes. When she stepped out of the dressing room, Aunt Melinda was waiting outside the door. She gave Alyssa the once-over, then smiled and nodded.

"Now, that's much better. You look like a normal schoolgirl at last," she said as she turned Alyssa around and examined her from the back.

Normal schoolgirl. The words cut into Alyssa. If she looked normal now, then what did her aunt think she looked like before? She tried to give her aunt the benefit of the doubt. Maybe the woman didn't mean to be rude, but still the words stung.

Aunt Melinda was leading Alyssa toward the shoe department when Uncle Steven and Dylan wandered in, looking lost.

"Aren't you gals ready yet? I'm starving," Uncle Steven grumbled.

"Oh, all right," Aunt Melinda said with a huff and seized a pair of blue shoes off the rack. "We'll get some more things later."

Alyssa had never felt more relieved than when she rushed out of the cold, refrigerated department store into the hot, muggy air. She pulled in deep gulps of the sea-scented air until her nerves calmed down.

Everyone climbed into the car, and Uncle Steven drove down Broadway, the main traffic artery running through the old city of Galveston. Huge Victorian mansions, some built before the Great

Hurricane of 1900, stood majestically to her left. Bright pink, red, and white oleanders, tall palms, and old, twisted live oaks growing in the esplanade cast their shadows onto the avenue.

They passed a cemetery dotted with tiny yellow daisies and with many somber aboveground tombs. Alyssa strained her eyes to see the top of the stone angel that guarded her mother's grave. She wanted to stop and show Dylan. He hadn't been there since the day she was buried, when he was only five. Alyssa tapped Uncle Steven on the shoulder and pointed.

"What is it, Alyssa?" he asked over his shoulder.

Alyssa pointed again. If he didn't slow, they would soon pass it.

"Do you know what she wants?" he whispered to his wife.

Aunt Melinda, busy helping Cecile remove tags from her new clothes, looked up.

"Did you say something, Steven?" she asked.

"I think Alyssa wants to stop at the ice cream parlor," Cecile suggested.

Alyssa let air escape between her teeth, then fell back against the car seat. Dylan stared at her through his dark-framed glasses. She pointed to the vanishing cemetery, too far away now, and quickly drew an angel on the notepad she had removed from her pocket. She wrote the word *Mom* across the angel's chest.

Dylan nodded. "Our mom is buried back there," he whispered. "I remember the angel."

A wave of relief and affection swept over Alyssa as she peered into the boy's sad brown eyes. She wanted to hug him, but she nodded instead.

Dylan studied the drawing on the paper a minute, took the pencil from his sister, and embellished the angel a little more. He tore the sheet of paper out, folded it neatly, and put it in his shirt pocket. Then he slumped back against the car seat and chewed his fingers.

Alyssa wondered how the boy had any fingernails left. He reminded her of a trapped animal gnawing off its own paw to escape. She had been wildly happy the day Dylan was born because she had wanted a little brother for so long. Somebody to play with in the ocean and on the beach. Someone to ride the horses with. Before the charter boat accident, Dylan had been her best pal. Sometimes Alyssa felt deep anger at her mother for dying and causing the family to separate. She shouldn't have gone off in the charter boat in such a bad storm. But deep inside, Alyssa knew it wasn't her mother's fault. It was her own.

Soon they had passed several stunning mansions and villas and the ornate turrets of Bishop's

Palace. Alyssa watched the tips of boat masts peeking over the tops of buildings a few blocks to her left at the piers. As always, she searched the face of every man she saw, hoping against all odds to catch a glimpse of her missing father.

When the car reached Seawall Boulevard at the far end of the city, Uncle Steven turned right and headed west.

"Why, look at those crazy teenagers out there trying to surf," Aunt Melinda said."Those big waves might smash them into the rock jetties or into the seawall. And just look at all those sightseers going in and out of the souvenir shops. You'd think they'd want to get away before the hurricane hits."

"Hurricanes are exciting, honey," Uncle Steven said, chuckling. "Didn't you see those TV cameramen back there? It's big news. And big business to the lumberyards, too." The pounding of hammers and the whine of buzz saws filled the air as shop owners nailed plywood over their windows. Some of them simply rolled down permanent metal covers.

To their left lay the seventeen-foot-high seawall, gallantly holding back the Gulf of Mexico, built because of the Great Hurricane of 1900. Along the sidewalk on top of the seawall, couples pedaled two-seater bicycles or covered surreys.

Teenagers roller-skated along the walk, in spite of the spray caused by waves crashing against great hunks of granite at the base of the wall. The sea had gradually crept up on the beach, preventing the usual horde of tourists from stretching out on towels or sitting under umbrellas every color of the rainbow.

Alyssa noticed a man with a shaggy beard staring back at her. Quickly she sat up. Of course, her father would probably have a beard now, or longer hair, or maybe some scars or a patch over one eye. And because of his amnesia, he wouldn't recognize her. She would have to be the one to take his hand and bring him home. She held her breath as the car drew closer to him, and she rolled the window down in spite of the air-conditioning. Suddenly the man held up a plastic-protected newspaper and smiled. His pale gray eyes twinkled as he shouted: "Hurricane Berta heading for Galveston! Get your souvenir paper right here!"

Alyssa let out a ragged sigh and slid back against the seat.

When the car stopped for a red light, Alyssa focused her eyes on a fixed spot on the beach far ahead and counted the slow-moving combers rolling in from far out on the gray ocean. They reminded her she had missed the noon news and the latest coordinates for Hurricane Berta. If the newspaper man was right, the storm must have turned slightly north and was now heading their way. The waves were coming in at the correct angle for that.

As they passed a souvenir shop bulging with seashells of every size and shape, along with racks of swimwear, Cecile begged for a new swimsuit.

Luckily, Uncle Steven was too hungry to stop. In a few moments they reached the restaurant. Alyssa felt uncomfortable in the expensive surroundings, but most of all she felt sorry for Dylan. He looked at the fish menu longingly, but Aunt Melinda made him order beef. Alyssa ordered a hamburger so he wouldn't feel alone, even though it brought another burst of giggles and whispers from Cecile.

After the meal, Cecile asked to visit a nearby ice cream parlor. Uncle Steven and Alyssa decided to cross the street and stand on the seawall to look at the churning sea.

For an instant, hardly more than a second, a memory flashed across Alyssa's mind. Three years ago the color of the sea and sky, the smell of fish and hamburgers and salty sea had all been the same as now. She had stood on the seawall while her parents bought flashlight batteries at a convenience store across the street. She remembered feeling the wind shove her chest and whip her hair back. She remembered seeing the outline of her skinny body showing through her dress. *Dress.* Yes, it had been a dress because they had been to church that morning. It was a Sunday, the day before the charter boat sank. The ocean had been exactly the same. Alyssa's father had bought each of them an ice cream bar, and her mother told her to get back inside the car to eat it, warning that the wind would pull the chocolate coating off. They had all laughed at her joke as Alyssa crawled back inside the car beside Dylan.

The memory was there one second, then it was gone. It wasn't a bad memory. It was kind of nice, except for knowing what happened the next day. Maybe if Alyssa very gradually retraced her steps from that Sunday and the next day, she would be able to recall everything.

Alyssa fell into deep concentration, but all she could remember happening the rest of that Sunday was the rosebushes swaying in the wind at their beach house in Pelican Village and her mother complaining about losing all the rose petals.

Back in Uncle Steven's car, while Cecile ate ice cream and chattered about her new clothes and trying out for the cheerleader squad when school started, Alyssa stared out the window. Soon the scenery changed from the busy boulevard to the country road that led to the west end of the island.

"Alyssa," Uncle Steven said over his shoulder as they approached the turnoff to Captain Mac's stables, "we'll be here until tomorrow boarding up our beach house. You're welcome to come over to spend the night with us. We've got plenty of bedrolls. Or you can share Cecile's bedroom."

"Mommy . . . ," Cecile protested, but Aunt Melinda hushed her up.

"Wouldn't that be fun, Alyssa? Spending the night at our house? It's so much cleaner than that old place where your grandfather lives. You and the children could play games all night. I'll cook pancakes for breakfast."

Alyssa vigorously shook her head and pointed to the little shack that had just come into view. Uncle Steven slowed the Mercedes and turned into the gravel driveway.

"Well," Aunt Melinda said, less cheerfully, "suit yourself. But at any rate, we'll drop back by tomorrow morning before we return to Houston. You'll need to be packed up and ready to go. You *do* know that you're coming to live with us, don't you? Captain Mac *did* tell you, didn't he?"

Alyssa swallowed hard. Even if there had been

nothing wrong with her voice, she would not have been able to talk. The lump in her throat was too large. She nodded because she didn't want them to think that her grandfather hadn't told her anything.

"Good. Monday we'll enroll you in school. You'll be going to the same middle school as Cecile. She's in the sixth grade now." Aunt Melinda turned to her daughter and patted her hand. Cecile lifted her chin and grinned. "You'll be in the seventh grade, Alyssa. Maybe you'll have the same lunch period. You'll at least get to ride together. Won't that be nice?"

Alyssa glanced at her cousin. Cecile rolled her eyes, crossed her arms, and with a heavy sigh, slumped back into the seat. Alyssa felt the same way, only worse. She could hardly stand being in the same family as Cecile, much less the same house and same school.

"We'll bring Cecile and Dylan over tomorrow morning," Aunt Melinda added. "Cecile wants to ride the horses. You can show her how while Steven and I finish closing up our beach house."

As the car stopped, Alyssa threw open the door and ran as fast as she could, passing under the noses of Captain Mac and Uncle D, who was carrying a sack of groceries.

"Here, now, lass! What's your hurry?" her grandfather called out. "Come here and see what I've got ye for your birthday."

But Alyssa didn't feel like seeing birthday presents. It was probably a five-dollar bill. He had given her money for her last two birthdays.

Alyssa slammed her bedroom door, then jerked off the blue jumpsuit and training bra. Red lines pressed into her shoulders and around her chest. She pulled out her oldest T-shirt and shorts, then dove onto the creaky bed. She smothered her head with the pillow and felt hot tears roll down her cheeks onto the sheet.

A few moments later Alyssa heard Uncle D's Cherokee driving away and the sound of Captain Mac fussing around in the kitchen putting away groceries. Then she heard the click of the phonograph and the squeak of his rocking chair as he sat down. Soon the high-pitched whine of bagpipes filled the house. The first song was "Amazing Grace," Captain Mac's favorite. Alyssa's father had bought the record many years ago. Alyssa used to love to sit at Captain Mac's feet and listen to the eerie strains rising and falling, sounding sometimes like a howling cat, sometimes like wind whistling through a conch shell.

After tiptoeing to the living room door, Alyssa watched the old man slumped in his chair, rocking gently. A thin gray line of smoke curled up from his pipe and hovered above his head before drifting out the open window. She heard her grandfather sniff, then saw him blow his nose on his crumpled white handkerchief.

She knew he would cry. Often he told her that the bagpipe tunes reminded him of Scotland and his parents, long dead. He usually played that record when he was feeling sad and thinking about dying.

The music filled Alyssa with sadness, too. Yet it wasn't as sad as the naval hymn that had been played at the seaside service for her missing father. She had tried to tell them that he was only missing, not dead; that his funeral service wasn't appropriate. She tried to tell the Coast Guard officers there that he had probably washed ashore down the coast and couldn't get home because he suffered from amnesia and didn't know his name or where he came from. But no one understood.

Quietly Alyssa retraced her steps to her bedroom and lay back down. She wasn't sure what she would do, but she did know one thing: if Captain Mac didn't need her as a granddaughter anymore, maybe she would show him that she didn't need him as a grandfather, either.

Chapter Seven

RENDEZVOUS

The next morning, Alyssa awoke to the sound of rosebushes scraping against her bedroom window. Her mother had planted them there many years ago to make Captain Mac's house look more cheerful. Her mother used to prune them back, but no one took care of them now. Only a few pale pink blossoms clung to the long, leggy limbs that danced in the wind.

It was still dark outside, and the east showed no signs of light. Alyssa retrieved a flashlight from under her bed and aimed its beam at an old clock shaped like a Spanish galleon. The dial was neatly set in the wooden hull beneath the dull metal sails that had become bent over the years. It had belonged to Alyssa's maternal grandfather, who had died a long time before she was born. He had not been a sailor, but the old clock fit right in with her collection of seashells and driftwood.

Usually all it took for Alyssa to awaken was the feel of morning—the pale light, the screaming sea gulls, and the fresh breeze bringing in the sweet fragrance of damp earth and wildflowers from the pastures. But today the air felt strange, as if it would smother her.

Alyssa slipped into clean clothes, then dragged out a faded navy blue duffel bag from under her bed. It had belonged to her father, left over from his years in the navy in Vietnam. Alyssa had not been born then, and he had not been married to her mother. When she was younger, Alyssa often crawled inside the duffel bag and drew the string tight, pretending to be a snail sticking its head out. Dylan would laugh and squeal with delight as he banged his sister's head with his rubber toys. Sometimes, when she got very mad, Alyssa stuffed the bag with clothes and waited for the right moment to run away from Captain Mac's. That moment never came before. Maybe this time would be different.

After a quick survey of her closet, Alyssa crammed some pants and tops into the bag. As she bumped into furniture in the dim light, she prayed that Captain Mac wouldn't wake up. She did not feel like facing him yet. At the end of the long, restless night, she had finally decided that she would not be there when Aunt Melinda and Uncle Steven came to pick her up. Whether or not she would run away for good, or just for a few days, she couldn't say. That would depend on how Captain Mac reacted.

Alyssa looked at her collections wistfully. It was hard to leave them behind. She wanted to take the old ship clock, but it was too heavy. She wondered who Captain Mac would give it to after she was gone. Probably Aunt Melinda, who more than likely would throw it away as junk because of the bent sails.

After packing the duffel bag with clothes, Alyssa slid it back under the bed. She would come for it later, after feeding the horses and returning her green boat to the secret cove.

For many minutes she struggled with the note, trying to explain why she was running away. Nothing sounded right. Finally she wished Captain Mac good luck in Scotland and told him not to worry about her. She placed the note on her chest of drawers under a glass storm lamp. Later, when she returned for the duffel bag, she would move the note to the kitchen table.

Alyssa slipped a notepad and stubby pencil into her pocket, then tiptoed to her grandfather's bedroom door. As usual the old man was sleeping on his back. His white beard stuck straight up and quivered each time he snored. Seeing him there so peaceful made Alyssa feel empty inside. She would be very lonely without him. He used to be so much fun. So many times they sat at the small Formica dinette table playing chess or checkers. The first time she beat him at chess, he pretended to stomp off mad, but later he baked her a tiny chocolate cake and bragged to his son how smart Alyssa was. Before the accident, they walked along the beach every day looking for seashells. He taught her how to find them in shallow water with her toes and how to remove the hermit crabs that often lived inside the empty shells. After a big storm, they always scoured the sands, praying to find a cowrie.

Why couldn't Captain Mac be like he was in the old days, Alyssa wondered. But since the charter boat accident, he didn't walk the beaches. He claimed it was his bad leg, which seemed to take a turn for the worse overnight. He didn't even care about the horses, or fishing, or boating. He had a permanent case of the doldrums.

Alyssa often thought about her grandfather and tried to figure out what had made him turn so unfriendly. She guessed he blamed her for the boat accident. And of course, he was mostly right about that. Even though she didn't remember what happened, she knew she must have caused the trouble. Otherwise why was her brain so reluctant to let her remember that day? The truth was probably even worse than what she imagined. Sometimes she was grateful for that lack of memory.

As Alyssa crept through the kitchen, she saw something on the dinette table—a small, round chocolate cake with thirteen yellow candles jabbed into it. Next to the cake was a tiny rectangular box crudely wrapped in pink tissue paper and tied with a crooked bow.

Alyssa felt sick inside. Her grandfather had gone to so much trouble and she had returned his kindness by being stubborn and mean. She unwrapped the matchbox and opened it. A golden heart-shaped locket winked in the flashlight beam. She had seen it in an old jewelry box. It had belonged to her grandmother and had been passed down from her great-grandmother, who wore it during the Great Hurricane of 1900. It came all the way from Europe and had become a symbol of good luck to the women in Alyssa's family.

Gently Alyssa pried the locket open and shined the light on two tiny photos, one of her mother and one of her father. Alyssa saw the crooked scissors marks and imagined Captain Mac's old trembling hands painstakingly cutting the faces out of a photograph.

Suddenly Alyssa felt awful for thinking of running away. She tiptoed back to her grandfather's room and stood beside his bed. Maybe she could trick her brain into letting her speak to him if she kept the words to a low whisper in his ear. With all her heart she wished she could tell him how sorry she was that her parents were gone. Sorry that she had acted like a wild savage for the past three years and caused him so much trouble.

The speech was all ready in Alyssa's head, but when she leaned over close to his face and tried to whisper, the same old feelings of dread and impending catastrophe made her stop. She gently stroked his white beard, then placed a soft kiss on his cheek, for old times' sake. His whiskers tickled her lips and, as always, smelled like pipe tobacco. He stopped snoring, smacked his lips a few times, then fell back to sleep.

After eating a piece of chocolate cake, Alyssa slipped out the back door and down to the stables.

As she stepped across the yard, she felt water slosh into her sneakers. The wind gusted and pushed her T-shirt against her ribs. Alyssa shined the flashlight beam toward the sea. It bounced off the creamy whitecap of a wave crashing onto the beach. As water sprayed her face, a sudden sense of urgency rushed through Alyssa's heart and she quickened her step.

The horses nickered and stuck their heads over the tops of their stalls. Their ears pricked up and their noses quivered softly as she flipped on the lights. Jo-Jo kicked the sides of his stall nervously, and Alyssa noticed that Stormy and Oscar had cribbed the doors overnight, leaving their teeth marks in the soft wood.

Alyssa turned on the radio for the six o'clock news. The weather service had changed its bulletin from a hurricane watch to a hurricane warning. Just as Alyssa had guessed, the new coordinates put Berta on a path toward Galveston. No one could say for sure if the storm would be a direct hit on the island or fall a few miles farther south. Either way would mean heavy rains and winds and high waters, especially on the low west end of the island, for the right side of a hurricane is always its worst.

After feeding the horses and putting them in the corral, Alyssa quickly raked out the dirty straw and manure from the stalls, then spread fresh hay and filled the water tubs.

She bridled Stormy and tied the long towrope of her green skiff around his chest. She had decided to take it back to the bayou and secure it to an old cottonwood tree that had withstood many years of hurricanes.

As Stormy crossed Termini Road, Alyssa glanced over her right shoulder toward the east. Through high, thin clouds that covered the whole sky, the eastern horizon glowed brick red. Overhead sea gulls laughed and acted crazy. The old saying "Red sky at dawning, Sailor take warning" flashed through her mind. She had heard her grandfather say those words many times, but never had she really understood them until now.

As they moved down the path toward the leeward side, mourning doves cooed soulfully on telephone wires overhead. Cattle in the fields grazed lazily, pausing to lift their heads and stare at Alyssa with blank expressions. White egrets stepped at their feet, picking at insects that the clumsy hooves stirred up.

The air felt heavy and full of foreboding. Except for the cry of sea gulls, it seemed too quiet, as if the insects and sparrows and blue jays had already left. Twice rabbits hopped out of Alyssa's way, and she found herself wondering how many of them would be alive after the hurricane had passed.

At the cove, Alyssa paused to look across the channel. A steady stream of car headlights moved over the causeway bridge that led from the island to the mainland. The evacuation had officially started yesterday and would continue until the Highway Patrol closed the bridge because of high winds or until the lower parts of Interstate 45 were under water. Some people always deserted the island at the first sign of a severe tropical storm, even if the weather service had not declared a hurricane warning or the mayor of Galveston had not called for an evacuation. Other people always stayed, even when he did.

The wind rattled the canes and grasses and reeds along the shoreline of the bayou. It was hard to believe that things could change so fast overnight. But Hurricane Berta was sounding her horn to warn them that she was on the way and nothing would stop her now.

Alyssa dismounted Stormy and dragged the skiff to the cottonwood tree. After tying a clove hitch, she wrapped the rope around the trunk several times, then finished it with a half-hitch and a slip half-hitch and cinched it tightly. She wanted to take no chances of the towrope coming loose.

Only if the tree itself blew away would the boat be lost.

She walked over the flats, stopping at the place where yesterday she had made the fire with Ty. Water poured into her sneakers. A great blue heron screamed angrily at her and flew low over the water until it landed on an old fence post sticking out of the bay. Usually that post jutted out about two feet. Now it was only a six-inch stub.

Alyssa was walking back to Stormy when she saw something red out of the corner of her eye. She stepped through some shrubs and weeds to get a better look. It was an old BMX dirt bike, with a torn seat and missing handlebar covers.

"Hey, Blondie, over here."

Alyssa jumped, then spun around. She put her hand over her heart and thumped her chest to let Ty know that he had startled her. The short boy laughed and pushed his way through the reeds. His legs were wet all the way to the ends of his shorts, and mud oozed over his high-topped sneakers. An Ace bandage peeped out of the top of one, and he wasn't limping as badly as he had the day before. Alyssa noticed a huge black bruise on the side of his face, right at the jawline.

"Are you ready to fish?" he asked as he pointed

to her green boat. "We can go out into the deeper water with your skiff. I brought plenty of bait." He held up a large plastic bag stuffed with small, bait-sized shrimp, the kind that were illegal at this time of the year since it was still closed shrimp season for one more day. The shrimpers were not supposed to use nets with small grids that caught young shrimp.

Alyssa wasn't in the mood for fishing, and with the hurricane getting closer every hour, she thought it would be wiser to go back. But Ty had gone to so much trouble to come here and looked so eager, she hated to turn him down. A few minutes of fishing wouldn't hurt. Besides, he was raving on and on about wanting to catch another flounder.

Alyssa thought about the day before and how good she had felt when she had said good-bye to Ty. She had made all kinds of plans for catching flounder—to bring a minnow seine, rubber boots, a gigging pole. And here she was again in sneakers with only dead shrimp for bait.

She led Ty to a place where it was still cool and the reeds grew close to the bay water. She leaned over and slapped the water with her flattened palm. It made a splat.

"Are you crazy?" Ty whispered, but she repeated the procedure until she heard a similar noise several yards away. Ty's eyes got wide and he scratched his head. She pointed to the spot where the noise had come from and they tiptoed there, making sure they were downstream, walking into the current.

Soon Alyssa saw the outline of the flat, brown, speckled fish with only its stalked eyes sticking out, each one moving separately from the other. Gently she cast out and let the bait drift over the flounder. The fish jumped up, seized the shrimp in its mouth, then after a few seconds, swallowed it. Alyssa handed the fishing rod to Ty and let him reel it in. She was glad they had caught one so fast; she really didn't want to fish any longer. Ty had already caught several redfish and a couple of trout before she arrived, so he was very happy now.

Seeing the flat fish squirming in Ty's net reminded Alyssa of the incident with her cousin and Dylan's coughing spell. Anger rushed over her at the memory of her fish being tossed away. She hoped that Ty wouldn't mention yesterday's flounder, but he must have been reading her mind.

"Well," he said, "did your grandpappy like that flounder I gave you?" He unconsciously stroked the bruised spot on the side of his jaw as he spoke.

Alyssa didn't want to lie, so she shrugged, hoping he would not probe any further.

"I'm glad somebody got good use out of it."
He moved his jaw back and forth, grimacing.

Alyssa reached over and touched the bruise
with her fingertip. She arched her eyebrows into
a question.

Ty shrugged and fidgeted uncomfortably. He
looked across the bay while fiddling with the fishing line. Then he sighed.

"It's nothing, Alyssa. Randon—that's my stepdaddy—was drinking, as usual. He was in a bad
mood because he got in a fight with Johnny, his
rigger. And he didn't like it because I'd skipped
out of repairing the nets. This ain't nothing—just
a little bruise. I was lucky he had a drinking buddy
over and didn't feel like really tearing into me.
And Momma cooked up the redfish we caught
real good, all hot and spicy just like Randon likes
it. His friend carried on about how good a cook
Momma was, so I got off easy, even without the
flounder."

A twinge of guilt crept through Alyssa as she
thought about the flounder being tossed on the
sand and left to rot because of Cecile and because
Aunt Melinda wanted to keep Dylan a helpless
baby forever.

Ty wanted to fish some more, but Alyssa let
him know that she couldn't stay any longer. It

was already eight o'clock. She wanted to get away before her aunt and uncle returned.

"I guess you're right, Blondie," Ty said as he reeled in his line for the last time. "It's getting too windy and really weird up there." He glanced up. The high cirrus clouds had moved on. Soon they would be completely replaced by the columns of thicker ones that were now hovering over the ocean to the south.

"Besides," he added, "I've got to get back and do some work on the shrimp boat before Randon comes back. He went into League City to buy some plywood to board up our rent-house. All the lumberyards around here already sold out. That's just like Randon—waiting till the last minute to do things, then getting mad as a bulldog when he can't find what he's looking for. We don't have many valuables in the house, but Randon's afraid the windows will break and looters will get in."

The two waded back to his bike, where Ty secured his tackle box and fishing rod onto the handlebars.

"Do you want to fish again sometime?" Ty asked as he pushed the red bike over to where Stormy was grazing. He patted Stormy's gray neck as if he'd known the horse for years.

Alyssa struggled with how to tell Ty that she

planned to run away. At least she had remembered to bring along her notepad and a pencil this time. She took it from her pocket and scribbled a few words. Ty's eyebrows, which were much darker than his dirty blond hair, crinkled and his lips puckered up as he tried to read her hasty handwriting.

"What's this mean? Are you going away for good?"

How could she explain? Ty would probably think she was crazy to pass up the chance to live with a rich family in a big house. Her uncle's house probably had bathrooms bigger than the living room in Ty's rent-house. He was still wearing the same Batman T-shirt and shorts that he had worn the day before, and they hadn't been washed. Neither had he.

Alyssa took the notepad back and scribbled "running away."

"Running away? I hope it's not because of what happened here yesterday. I mean, did you get into trouble for fishing with me? I guess your grandpappy doesn't approve of me . . . Nobody ever does." He stared at the ground, then pivoted and started to walk away.

Alyssa grabbed his arm and shook her head. It was too hard to explain about her grandfather missing Scotland and his bum leg and wanting to send her to Houston. She quickly scratched on the notepad: "Grandpa moving away—selling horses."

Ty nodded. "I get it. So he's moving and you don't want to live anywhere else, so you're running away. I bet he wants to move someplace where there's no hurricanes."

Alyssa stared at Ty's blue eyes, amazed at his perception.

"Well, don't worry," he said as he helped her up onto Stormy. "After this one blows over, he'll probably change his mind. At least until the next one stirs up in the Gulf. A lot of folks on Galveston feel that way. Say, why don't you come to visit me on our shrimp boat for a little while? My mom can cook up flounder out of this world. She uses Cajun spices and stuff like that. She's part French, you know. So was my real daddy."

Alyssa hesitated a long time. Ty shook one of her feet. "Come on, girl. Randon won't be back for a couple of hours. Let's go put your horse back in the stables and I'll pump you on my handlebars. It's not far from here. Our shrimp boat's docked at that little landing at the end of Eight Mile Road for right now. We're having trouble with the bilge pump and had to work on it a couple of days."

Alyssa didn't indicate yes, but she didn't indicate no, either. She ran all prospects through her mind and finally decided that if she did run away, Ty's shrimp boat was just about as good a place as any to go.

While she rode Stormy, Ty pedaled his bike down the narrow side road. The pastures buzzed with activity now as farmers loaded up their more valuable livestock, such as horses and prized bulls, to haul them to the safety of the mainland. One man tried to get his three longhorn steers into a cattle trailer. The animals stubbornly bowed their heads and planted their hooves into the ground as they snorted and bellowed. Other farmers would leave their cattle in the pastures and pray for the best.

On a little man-made hill, an elderly couple carried blankets and food into a windowless storm shelter built forty years ago by a rich farmer. About twenty yards away from it, on another little hill, stood a barn built for his prize cows. Both the pasture and the buildings had been abandoned, silent and empty except during severe storms when a few local residents used the structures for storage and shelter.

Soon Captain Mac's house and stables came into view. At the back end of the pasture, Ty and Alyssa stopped.

"Uh-oh, looks like you've got some customers," Ty said. "Who'd want to ride horses on a day like this? Must be some rich folks. Look at that Mercedes." He whistled low.

Alyssa sighed, then glanced at her watch. It wasn't even nine o'clock yet. She hadn't expected her relatives this early. Now she wouldn't be able to sneak in and get her duffel bag from under the bed. She would have to show Cecile and Dylan how to ride the horses and somehow get away before her aunt and uncle returned to take her to Houston.

Alyssa watched Cecile climb out of the car, dressed in what she guessed to be real riding clothes, even though the pants and top looked like something to be worn at a fashion show. Poor Dylan, Alyssa thought. She could see his knobby knees all the way from where she was sitting. And his face looked as white as the sand.

Alyssa flipped open her notepad and wrote: "Not customers. Relatives. Come to stables with me. *Please*."

"Okay, but just a little while. Man, I didn't know you had such rich relatives, Blondie. You sure are lucky."

Alyssa didn't respond, but as they approached the group of people standing in the yard staring at them, she didn't feel lucky at all.

Chapter Eight

A MISUNDER-

STANDING

The adults stood at the back porch and the children lingered near the corral. Alyssa had a feeling that she was going to get into trouble all over again for not being there when they arrived. Once again her shoes were caked with mud and sand, but at least her clothes were clean today.

While Alyssa tied Stormy to a post, Ty leaned his bicycle against the corral fence. Everyone stared at the twosome as they strolled toward the house.

"Don't worry," Ty whispered as he patted Alyssa's shoulder. "You won't get into trouble. Let me do all the talking." When he realized what he'd said, he grinned and winked. With his shoulders squared and his chin high, the compact boy sauntered up to the porch.

"Morning," he said to Captain Mac, undaunted by the scowling face above him. "I'm Ty DuVal, Alyssa's fishing buddy. It's a pleasure to meet you, sir. Your granddaughter has told me all about you. We brought you some fish, sir."

Captain Mac's eyebrows shot up. "Oh? Is it true, lass? Have ye been talkin' to this lad?"

Alyssa squirmed and felt the color rush from her face. What was Ty doing? If Captain Mac thought she talked to Ty, but not to adults, she truly would be in trouble.

Ty smiled and shook his head.

"Of course I don't mean that she actually spoke about you using words. But there are lots of other ways to communicate besides talking. Right, Alyssa?"

All eyes turned to Alyssa. She nodded.

"It looks like you might need help at the stables now and then. I'd be glad to come by after school and on weekends, if you don't mind, sir. I love horses." Ty winked at Alyssa. She was stunned that he was saying all this, and she couldn't help remembering the first time he'd tried to ride Stormy. Alyssa smiled at the thought, but her grandfather did not share her feelings. His face remained stern.

"There was a day when I would have taken up your offer, laddie. But I'm sellin' the wee horses and closin' down the stables. I'm expectin' a man from Freeport to arrive any time now to buy them and haul them off before the storm hits. But you're welcome to groom them up so they'll look all ship-shape when he comes by. And thanks for the fish."

Alyssa's heart sank. This was the first time that her grandfather had actually admitted to her aloud that he was serious about selling the horses. Until now she had hoped that somehow he didn't really mean what he said. She turned away to keep the adults from seeing the tears well up in her eyes. As she started to walk away, she felt Ty's hand on her shoulder.

"Sorry about the horses," he said softly. "Wish there was something I could do. I'll keep thinking while I'm cleaning these fish for your grandpappy."

Alyssa fought back more tears as she walked to the tack room at the back of the stables. A whiff of hoof polish and saddle soap filled the air as she opened the door and took out a curry comb and brush.

As Alyssa walked to the corral, she noticed that

Cecile was pulling up Johnson grass and feeding it to Stormy through the rails. Not wanting the sharp blades to cut the horse's tongue, Alyssa jerked the grass from her cousin's hand and shook her head. Cecile glared, then tossed her dark curls and reached for a bull nettle plant growing next to the fence. Before Alyssa could stop her, Cecile had yanked the plant with both hands.

With a screech, Cecile dropped the weed and scratched her hands. Tears popped up as she scratched harder. Red welts rose on her palms, and she ran screaming to the house. Alyssa turned around, bumping into Dylan. The boy whimpered and ran after Cecile.

Alyssa saw her aunt stomping across the yard, her sandaled feet making dimples in the sand. Uncle Steven followed close behind, his face furrowed with concern.

"What did you do to Cecile?" Aunt Melinda demanded. "Just look at her hands." She forced Cecile to hold up her welt-covered hands.

Alyssa pointed to the bull nettle laying in the sand where Cecile had dropped it. Even a dumb animal knew better than to bother that plant. Anybody should have been able to tell that it was covered with sticky barbs.

Aunt Melinda looked confused as she turned to her husband.

"What's she trying to say?" she asked.

He leaned over, nudged the plant with the toe of his suede shoe, and kicked it aside.

"It's a bull nettle, honey. It causes itching, but it'll go away pretty soon. Now, you children need to stay away from all these weeds. You don't know what might be poisonous or not. And I imagine there are a lot of snakes around here, too. Right, Alyssa?"

Alyssa nodded as she looked into his kind eyes. Sometimes she wondered why he had ever married Aunt Melinda. She seemed the opposite of Uncle Steven in every way. He was so kind and patient and didn't get easily upset over every little thing. He reminded Alyssa of her father, in a way. It was strange that Aunt Melinda was the one who was blood kin to her and Uncle Steven wasn't. She wished it were the other way around.

"Oh, all right," Aunt Melinda said. "But, Alyssa, you need to warn Cecile and Dylan if they start to get into something that can hurt them. They don't know anything about plants and animals like you do. You never know what Dylan might be allergic to. You're going to have to be more responsible for him and Cecile."

A smug look crept across Cecile's face. Dylan hid behind his aunt's skirt, his fingers in his mouth. Only Uncle Steven acted as if he understood how

Alyssa felt. He put his big hands—browned from years of working outside collecting rocks and soil samples—on her shoulders.

"It's all right, Alyssa. I know it wasn't your fault. But just remember that these guys are city slickers. How about showing them how to ride the horses? But pick a real gentle one." He smiled and winked.

Alyssa returned to the stables and brought back a saddle and bridle. She saddled up Oscar, a black-and-white pinto that was gentle and reliable. In a little while, after Cecile had ridden around the pen a few times and grew confident, Aunt Melinda and Uncle Steven returned to their car and drove off. Dylan stared after the car, biting on his nails more intensely than before. He seemed on the verge of crying. Alyssa tried to get him to ride Skippy, the oldest, most gentle mare in the stable. She never ran anymore. But Dylan shook his head and hugged a fence post, refusing to come inside the corral.

"I'm allergic to horses," he said in a shaky voice.

Ty, who was cleaning fish behind the stables, stopped what he was doing. He walked over to Dylan, still holding the knife in one hand.

"Hey, come over here and help me clean these fish? No? Then, why don't you help me brush down old Trigger over there. It'll be fun." He pointed the knife toward Stormy.

Dylan shook his head. "Aunt Melinda says animals might make me sick. Their hair might get in my nose and make me cough. I might die."

"*Hmm*, I see." Ty scratched his head. "Okay, then how about me and you going for a bike ride down the beach? You look bored standing here with nothing to do, Curly." He tousled Dylan's brown curls.

Dylan eyed the red bike leaning against the fence. Then he sighed.

"Aunt Melinda won't let me ride a bike on the beach. She says dirt will make me cough. Besides, I don't know how to ride one."

Ty crinkled his eyebrows, then looked at Alyssa. She shrugged. There was no point in trying to understand her brother, she thought. As far as she could tell, he should be living in a glass cage. At the rate he was going, he would be in one pretty soon.

"Why, the beach isn't the same as dirt," Ty said. "Hasn't anyone ever explained that to you, Curly? Wait here while I put these fish in the fridge for your grandpappy."

A few minutes later, Ty returned. He steered Dylan to the red bike and helped the boy up. At first Dylan had an expression of terror plastered on his face, but as Ty held on to the seat and handlebars and broke into a trot, the young boy's face lit up with a bright smile.

Alyssa grunted in disbelief as the two vanished down the beach. She picked up the curry comb and brushed the shiny chestnut coat of Jo-Jo, the fastest and biggest horse. Only their experienced customers were allowed to ride him.

Cecile stared after Dylan, a look of scorn on her face. Suddenly she jerked the reins hard, almost making Oscar rear up.

"This is too boring," she announced. "I want to ride down the beach."

At the same time that Alyssa turned around to tell her cousin no, she heard the squeaking metal gate and the jingle of chains. Alyssa groaned and reached for the notepad in her pocket. She had just scribbled the words "no running" when Cecile jabbed her heels into Oscar's ribs. He bolted like a dart.

There was nothing for Alyssa to do except leap up onto Jo-Jo and go after her cousin. By the time Alyssa reached the corral gate, it had already swung shut. As she opened the gate, she heard Ty shout: "Ride 'em, cowgirl!" Dylan laughed hysterically as he watched first Cecile, then Alyssa charge down the beach.

It only took a couple of minutes for Cecile's

first exhilarating peals of laughter to turn into screams of horror when she realized she couldn't make the horse stop. Her plump bottom slapped up and down in the saddle because she didn't know how to settle her weight.

Cecile was pretty far ahead of Alyssa, heading straight for a low fence that marked the boundary between the public beach and the land that belonged to a county park. Oscar was a good horse and very loyal to his rider. If he thought that Cecile was kicking him on purpose to make him run, he would go until he dropped dead. And he would gladly jump over the fence if he thought that was what was expected of him.

Alyssa gritted her teeth as she leaned down low on Jo-Jo's back. Pretty soon the wind brought tears to her eyes and everything ahead blurred. She saw Cecile's white blouse and Oscar's spotted legs suddenly sailing over the fence. Cecile's screams sounded like those of someone on a roller coaster, then it was very quiet except for the thunder of Jo-Jo's hooves and the roar of the ocean surf.

Alyssa pulled Jo-Jo to a halt at the fence. Cecile lay with her face in the sand, sobbing. A wave rolled in, casting white foam on her new sneakers. Oscar had wandered back to investigate. His pink nose quivered softly on Cecile's back as he nudged her.

"Get away!" She screamed so loudly that Oscar jerked his head up and trotted a few yards away. He whinnied and blew air through his nostrils.

Alyssa climbed over the fence and tried to help Cecile up, but the girl pushed her away. When Cecile tried to hit her cousin with her left hand, she grimaced and clasped her arm.

"My arm!" she cried. "I think my arm is broken. Go get a doctor. Hurry."

Alyssa whistled to Oscar, whose brown eyes were still sad and confused looking.

"Get that . . . that stupid animal away from me," Cecile yelled. "He should be sent to the glue factory or shot for what he did to me."

Alyssa's instincts were to drop her cousin in the sand, but she bit her lip and forced herself to help the girl back onto Oscar's back. Cecile resisted at first but finally climbed back into the saddle. Alyssa remounted Jo-Jo and led Oscar around the fence and back to Captain Mac's house.

Uncle D had just driven up and now stood beside Captain Mac on the back porch, watching the two girls.

"I need a doctor," Cecile whined pathetically. "Somebody call an ambulance."

"What in thunderation happened, lass?" Captain Mac asked as Uncle D and Ty helped Cecile off the horse.

"It's all Alyssa's fault," Cecile sobbed. "Daddy told her to pick a gentle horse, but she picked that old wild stallion. He ran away with me and I couldn't stop him. Then he jumped over a fence and knocked me off. She knew I didn't know how to ride. She should have picked a gentle horse. Now my arm's going to be in a cast when school starts. I won't be able to be in the tryouts." The tears rolled down her face as she opened her mouth wide and bellowed.

Captain Mac stared at Alyssa but said nothing. He turned around and limped back inside the house, following Uncle D, who was carrying Cecile. It was no easy task for the old man since he wasn't all that strong and she wasn't all that skinny.

Alyssa glanced down at Dylan, who sat on the bottom porch step. A sly little smile lingered on his lips. Whether it was because Cecile was in pain or because Alyssa was in trouble, she wasn't sure. Maybe it was for both reasons. After a minute, Dylan hopped to his feet, took Ty's hand, and pulled him back toward the red bike.

"Let's ride some more," he said cheerfully as he pushed the bike toward the beach.

It wasn't long before the silver Mercedes pulled into the driveway. Everything went just as Alyssa had expected. She was glad she had decided to hide under the bed before they arrived. She didn't like tight places, but with the door open she could get a good view of the living room, where all the adults had gathered around the wailing Cecile.

By the time her aunt and uncle and Captain Mac and even Uncle D had finished arguing and yelling, Alyssa's own throat was sore just thinking of all the noise.

"It wasn't the lassie's fault. Oscar is a gentle horse. I don't know what got into him to make him run like that," Captain Mac said.

"It's settled," Aunt Melinda interrupted sharply, and held up her hand. "Steven and I don't want to hear another word, Captain Mac. That child needs psychiatric treatment, and that's all there is to it. She's cruel and irresponsible. I won't have her in *my* house threatening *my* daughter. I don't care if she is my sister's child. I cannot risk the safety of my own child. And she's a bad influence on Dylan, too. If we hadn't been there when she put that fish in his face, he might have had a terrible allergic reaction. He might have . . ." She paused to draw in a deep breath.

"Now, Melinda, don't get yourself all upset," Uncle Steven said softly. "Nothing happened to Dylan."

"Well . . . maybe she would be better off in an institution."

Alyssa watched Uncle Steven's brown Hush Puppies as he paced back and forth past the opened bedroom door. He stopped, and she imagined him looking into her room and seeing the neat rows of seashells and varnished driftwood.

"Melinda . . . we promised to take care of her at least for a little while. I'll not go back on my word. We have to give her a chance. Think about Captain Mac here. His leg is getting so bad he can't take care of her anymore. We can't let her become a ward of the state. It's not moral."

Alyssa heard her aunt's heavy sigh. Then she heard a loud slam as something hit the floor.

"All right, all right, Steven, you win. But I will only let Alyssa stay with us on the condition that she sees a psychiatrist immediately. And you must agree to do whatever he recommends."

"Okay, honey, I agree," he said in a soothing voice. "Everything will be all right. Don't get all upset."

Alyssa rolled onto her back and stared up at

the coils of springs poking through the wooden slats of her bed. Any thoughts she had of things working out between herself and her relatives fled from her mind at that moment. She liked Uncle Steven, but Aunt Melinda and Cecile and even her own brother didn't want her around. They probably never would, she thought. And her grandfather couldn't raise her anymore, even if he wanted to. Which he probably didn't.

When Alyssa had packed her duffel bag that morning, she wasn't really certain that she would run away. It was just something that she did to make her feel that she was taking action. But now she had no doubts that it was the only solution. She would wait until after everyone left, and Captain Mac wasn't looking, then she would make her move.

Chapter Nine

ON THE

SHRIMP

BOAT

After the adults had gone outside to the car, Alyssa crawled from under her bed and slipped out through the window. Peering around the corner of the house, she watched Uncle Steven place Cecile into the back seat of the Mercedes. Cecile whimpered as Aunt Melinda scooted beside her and put a damp washcloth against her forehead.

"Dylan!" Uncle Steven motioned Dylan and Ty over to the car. "We're taking Cecile to the doctor's office. Do you want to wait here?"

"Yes," Dylan said timidly, glancing up at Ty.

"Curly is turning out to be a champion biker," Ty said with a wink. "This time next year, he'll be in the Tour de France."

"That's amazing," Uncle Steven said and scratched his head. "Melinda, did you hear that? Dylan is riding a bike. I thought he was afraid of bicycles."

"Oh, no, you mustn't let him ride," Aunt Melinda said as she poked her head out of the window. "The dirt will make him get a coughing spell. Dylan, do you hear me? No more bike riding! Maybe you'd better come along with us and get an allergy shot."

"No!" Dylan said, and scooted behind Ty, then stuck his fingers in his mouth and chewed on his knuckles.

"Oh, let the boy stay," Uncle Steven said. "He'll be careful. And Ty will watch out for him, won't you?"

Ty grinned. "Sure. I've got a little sister his age. I taught her how to ride just last week. It's no problem."

Aunt Melinda didn't seem satisfied with that answer. She was about to protest again, but Uncle Steven broke in.

"Where's the nearest doctor, Captain Mac?"

Alyssa's grandfather limped to the car and leaned on the door.

"Dr. Reeves is a few miles down the road. He's the one I've been usin' for ten years now. Would ye mind if I rode along with ye, Stevie? My leg is hurtin' something fierce today. I'd like Dr. Reeves to take a look at it and maybe change my prescription."

"Sure, sure," Uncle Steven said as he got out and helped Captain Mac climb into the passenger seat. After he got settled in, the old man turned his head and stared exactly where Alyssa was hiding.

"Come out in the open, lassie. No one's goin' to chastise ye for what happened. We know it was an accident."

Alyssa stepped from behind the wall and joined Ty and Dylan.

"Watch after your little brother while we're gone," Aunt Melinda added. "It'll probably take a couple of hours. When we get back, we'll leave for Houston. Be sure to have everything packed and ready to go."

Uncle D said good-bye then got into his Cherokee and followed them out of the driveway to Termini Road. All three of the children sighed in relief.

"What a pain that girl is," Ty said. "I feel sorry for Curly having to live with her. I bet you never get to sleep with her motor mouth whining all the time."

Dylan nodded then ran to the red bike and picked it up off the sand. "Let's ride some more, Ty."

Ty shook his head. "Sorry, but I've got to get back to the shrimp boat. I forgot I have to repair some nets before my stepdaddy comes back. I don't want to give him an excuse to punch me again." He rubbed his chin slowly.

"You live on a boat?" Dylan asked.

"Sometimes. While we're out at sea during the summers."

"Can I see your boat? Please?" The boy looked up with pleading eyes. For the first time, Alyssa noticed that his brown eyes didn't look so sad behind the dark-rimmed glasses. And his cheeks had a little color from the hour he had spent playing outside.

"Well, sure, why not. It's not very far. Why don't both of you come?"

Dylan clapped his hands, but Alyssa pointed to the horses and the overhead sign that read Horses for Rent. Ty laughed.

"Do you really think customers will come today? They'd have to be crazy. It's starting to sprinkle already."

He was right. The higher columns of cumulus clouds from over the ocean had been moving closer all morning, broken with occasional strips of lighter sky. The low nimbus clouds that bore most of the hurricane's rain and wind and fury were still over a hundred miles away, slowly moving toward them like a wall of dull gray gloom. The blazing ninety-two-degree heat of the day before had cooled down to eighty-eight degrees, and the wind was getting stronger.

"Look, this is the last time I'll get to see you, Blondie. I'm sure Randon will move the boat to a higher pier or go up the Intracoastal Canal to Louisiana. I may not be back for days. If you're moving away, you won't be here when I get back."

"She doesn't have to come," Dylan asserted. "Just take me on your bike."

Dylan scrambled onto the makeshift passenger seat fitted over the back wheel. Alyssa thought about the peace and quiet she would have with everyone gone. It was the perfect time to run away. She wouldn't have to wait until later when it was raining and more dangerous. But something prevented her from letting Dylan go off alone. Maybe he was strange-acting, but he was still her baby brother and she had promised to look after him.

She shrugged and nodded. She decided she would let Dylan look at Ty's boat for a few minutes, then hurry back home. They should be able to return easily before the doctor finished with Cecile's arm and Captain Mac's leg.

"Great," said Ty, slapping hands with Dylan. "Didn't I see an old bike in the stables?" he asked Alyssa. "Maybe Curly could ride it."

Alyssa had almost forgotten about the bicycle. It had been her first one, a present on her sixth birthday. It was too small for her now, but just right for Dylan's short legs.

While Ty pumped up the tires, Alyssa returned to the house and got rain slickers for herself and Dylan, and Captain Mac's giant black umbrella. The first band of rain clouds on the hurricane's outermost edge would arrive before too long. It wouldn't be so bad, just like a sudden summer thunderstorm, and the wind wouldn't be deadly. They still had several hours before the weather got really bad. But from here on, the day would be wet and blustery. Not great conditions for riding bikes.

Dylan didn't like the idea of riding a girl's pink bicycle, but Ty convinced him that it was the only way that all three of them could get to his boat. Dylan protested but soon discovered that he liked the smaller bike better than Ty's because it was easier to handle.

After several minutes of pedaling, mud covered Dylan's new sneakers and dirty water had splattered all over his clean white shirt. Alyssa knew that when Aunt Melinda saw him, she would have a heart attack.

Palm trees swayed above them, and oleander bushes rustled along the side of the road. Cars and pickups hauling boats passed, some honking impatiently when the traffic jammed at an intersection. When Alyssa saw Holly's brown geodesic dome house up ahead on the corner, she knew they were at the turnoff. They were making good time and would reach the landing shortly.

Rain began to fall. Alyssa popped open the umbrella and held it over herself and Ty while she clung to his waist with her free hand. With the sky getting so gloomy and the wind picking up, Alyssa had a strange feeling that she was making a terrible mistake by going to the shrimp boat. It wasn't very far away, but suppose the bike tires blew out, or Dylan fell off and broke his arm? So many things could happen. But it was too late to turn back. The landing was up ahead.

"We're almost there," Ty shouted over his shoulder. "It's that big white boat with the red trim."

The shrimp boat stood fifty feet long, bigger than the small thirty-footers that stuck to the bay waters. But on the other hand, she wasn't as big as the sixty- or hundred-footers that shrimped out in the open seas. Her outriggers stuck up like praying hands and her loose nets swayed softly in the wind like a woman's hair. A black diesel smokestack jutted from the engine room.

Ty chained the bikes to a metal pole. Alyssa's chain still had the key in the lock, left there from the last time she had ridden the bike many years ago.

The brief rain shower had stopped, leaving a layer of glistening water on the deck.

"Come on up," Ty said as he lifted Dylan and planted him on the deck, then gave Alyssa a helping hand as she crossed the wet plank. The boat rocked roughly, smacking against the pilings.

"Momma!" Ty shouted as he pushed Alyssa and Dylan toward the cabin. A thin, sickly woman with a pale face and a tired expression came to the door. She held a frying pan in one hand and a dishrag in the other. Her eyes, surrounded by dark circles, were the same morning glory blue as Ty's.

"Momma, this is Alyssa, the girl I told you about last night. And this is her brother, Dylan. They've never been on a shrimp boat. I told them they could visit a while, okay?"

The woman didn't smile, and her lips seemed to turn down more at the corners. She sighed and pushed back a stray curl of mousy brown hair from her skinny face.

"Looks like I don't have much say in what you do lately, Tybalt. But take my advice and get them gone before Randon comes back. And for mercy's sake, don't forget to finish repairing them nets."

"Thanks, Momma. You're a kind soul." He placed a soft kiss on her cheek. The woman smiled weakly and Alyssa had the feeling that it was the most the woman ever smiled. Just looking at her made Alyssa feel tired.

Ty led Alyssa and Dylan through the cabin, where his mother had been cleaning fish. The tiniest gas stove and refrigerator Alyssa had ever seen took up one side of the room and a homemade padded bench took up the other. A couple of bar stools were screwed down next to a Formica-covered snack bar. Everything smelled greasy and fishy, not like her father's charter boat, which had always been kept spotless and fresh. She expected Dylan to turn green and start wheezing at any second. But her brother seemed satisfied to follow Ty around like a puppy.

"Come on below and meet my little sisters." Ty opened a short door and pointed at two steps leading below deck. All Alyssa could see were the edges of two bunk beds and some ice chests. Two girls with dingy brown hair and blue eyes like

Ty's sat on the lower berth playing a game of Monopoly. The beds hadn't been made up and the curtains over the portholes hung like dirty rags. The floor felt sticky under Alyssa's feet. Her father's boat had been a palace compared to this. Even down below, the smell of fish and shrimp oozed out of every corner.

As the boat rocked with a sudden gust of wind, Alyssa felt her head go light. She had not been below deck of a boat in three years. She had not even set foot above deck. She felt all queasy, but not because she was seasick. She had been on the ocean dozens of times and even rough waters had not made her nauseated. It was something else. Something deep inside her that was scratching and gnawing like a trapped animal trying to get out of a cage. A memory surged over her, almost making her lose her balance. She wanted to go back up for fresh air, but the girls looked at her with curious eyes and she couldn't let them think she was a landlubber.

Alyssa forced the lump back down her throat and pretended that nothing was wrong. She watched Ty kid around and try to mess up his sisters' board game. The girls teased him a lot, too. Even though he was the oldest, he was shorter than Suzanne, who was about eleven years old. She didn't say much or smile much, either. Once when she did smile, Alyssa noticed that her teeth were crooked and awful looking, so she imagined that was why Suzanne was so quiet.

The younger girl, Marie, chattered constantly and asked Alyssa a million questions. Ty tried to explain that Alyssa couldn't speak, but Marie kept on firing away. Sometimes Alyssa wrote her answers on her notepad, other times she used hand gestures to communicate. Marie thought this was great fun, like a game of charades. She even said she wished she were mute, too. Then she braided Alyssa's long blond hair and held her hand.

Suzanne helped them take off their rain slickers and begged them to play a game of Monopoly. Alyssa shook her head, but she was outnumbered. When Dylan began to win the game, the girls teased him by pulling his hair and Ty threw his rolled-up socks at the miniature plastic houses and hotels. Suddenly there was a commotion topside. Then a motor started up with a roar, making the whole boat vibrate.

"Shoot!" Ty bolted for the door. "Randon's home!"

The girls scrambled frantically to put the game pieces back into the tattered cardboard box.

"Randon doesn't like us playing games," Marie

whispered as she shoved the box under the mattress of the upper bunk.

Ty bounded up the steps and closed the door behind him. His sisters raced across the tiny room and pressed their ears to the wooden door. Alyssa's heart pounded as she felt the boat slowly moving and the air filling with the stench of diesel smoke and the sound of the popping motor. She glanced at the wall clock and saw that it was almost noon. She couldn't believe they had been on the boat over an hour. Aunt Melinda and Uncle Steven might be back from the doctor's office by now. Aunt Melinda would be hysterical when she discovered that Dylan was missing. She might not care about Alyssa, but she would probably call the police about Dylan.

Alyssa scooted to the porthole and drew back a flimsy curtain. They were gliding past the landing and heading across West Bay toward the causeway bridge. The buoys marking the boundaries of the deep Intracoastal Canal bobbed wildly in the choppy water ahead of them. It wasn't very deep where they were now. She could easily wade or swim to shore. But she wasn't sure about Dylan. His little face grew paler as he moved close to Alyssa and stuck his fingers in his mouth.

Alyssa got up and tried to pull Suzanne and

Marie away from the door so she could open it, but they held her back.

"Shh," Suzanne whispered, putting her finger over her lips. "Don't make any noise."

"Has Randon been drinking?" Marie whimpered.

"I don't know . . . maybe not."

Suddenly a loud pop and a cry rose from the deck. Ty shouted, and his mother screamed and pleaded.

"He's really letting Momma have it," Marie said in a trembling voice. Tears rolled down her cheeks. Suzanne's eyes were dry, but her knuckles turned white as she gripped the door handle. Another pop rang out. Suzanne pulled Marie close to her.

"Alyssa, what's happening?" Dylan asked timidly as he tugged his sister's T-shirt. She looked down into his big, sad eyes. She wished she could tell him something comforting, but she knew they were not safe. She scribbled a message on her notepad, telling him not to worry, but he didn't seem convinced. Alyssa knew they had to get off the boat before they got out too far.

"I told you to fix the nets, you good-for-nothing, lazy piece of trash," a man shouted angrily.

Alyssa couldn't stand it another minute. She

pushed Suzanne with all her strength and grabbed the door handle. Suzanne and Marie pounced on Alyssa and pulled her back.

"No!" Suzanne pleaded in a harsh whisper. "He's drunk. If you go up there he's liable to beat you silly. And he'll get even madder at Ty. The best thing to do is just hide down here until he's sleeping it off. He'll be dead to the world then."

Alyssa shook her head. She had no intention of sitting there as if nothing were happening. She scuffled with Suzanne over the door handle. Suddenly the door began to move. The girls scattered like frightened rabbits. Dylan stepped back. Everyone stared at the steps.

It was Ty's mother. She walked down slowly, holding the side of her face. She didn't say a word but headed straight for the little bathroom. She picked up a washrag, rinsed it off, and pressed it to her lip. When she faced the children, they saw that one eye was red and puffed up until it was almost shut and her lip was busted.

"You girls tidy up a little," she said in a tight, small voice. "I've got to fix Randon's lunch."

Ty's mother returned upstairs to the kitchenette. Through the partially opened door, Alyssa watched her pick up a fish and slap it onto the Formica countertop. Her butcher knife came down with a fast, hard chop and the fish head

155

dropped into the metal sink. Then she jabbed its stomach and ripped it open and jerked out the innards.

The door remained open a crack and Alyssa could hear Ty and his stepfather arguing, but not as loudly as before. She decided to take a chance and go up the steps, but before she reached the top, Ty's face suddenly loomed in the doorway above. His cheeks burned red and a spot of drying blood clung to one nostril. He clenched his jaws firmly as he grabbed the door.

"Stay down below until I say it's safe," he said in a low voice. He started to close the door, then paused. He swallowed hard several times. "Look, Blondie, Curly . . . I . . . I'm sorry about this." He slammed the door.

Suzanne took Alyssa's hand and led her to the bunk bed. "Let's just play charades or something," she whispered. "Don't worry, Randon will go to sleep pretty soon and we'll be all right. He ain't so bad when he's sober." She squeezed Alyssa's hand and forced a crooked smile.

"Sissy," Marie said in a tiny voice, not as shaky as it had been before, "where are we going? Did Randon board up the rent-house?"

Suzanne pushed back her stringy, limp hair. "I heard him say he couldn't find any plywood. Looked for hours. Then some guys at the bar made fun of him for waiting so late to board up. He got into a fistfight."

"Guess that's why he's in such a bad mood."

"Yeah. I heard him tell Momma we're going to Louisiana. That's where Uncle Jackson lives— in Lake Charles. Remember, we went there last Christmas."

Alyssa felt dizzy and nauseous all of a sudden. Lake Charles was a long way up the coastline. She peeked out the porthole again. They were passing under the causeway bridge now. Up ahead lay Pelican Island. The choppy waves, stirred by the wind, slapped against the hull of the shrimp boat, making it slow going.

Suddenly the boat leaned as it turned starboard and headed toward the deep waters of the Galveston Channel. If Randon was going to Louisiana, he wasn't taking the direct route of the Intracoastal Canal, the narrow, dredged waterway that ran along the coast from Texas to Florida. That would have been a quick and safe way to go in such bad weather.

Alyssa watched the scenery go by. A few minutes later, the boat threaded its way between small Pelican Island and Galveston Island. Most of the slots at the piers were empty and the ferry had already closed down. At the tip of the larger island several wade fishermen cast out over the choppy waves. Tourists huddled at the end of Seawall Boulevard looking at the ocean's angry waves.

Alyssa moved across the room and looked out the other porthole. When she spotted the old abandoned lighthouse on Bolivar Peninsula, she thought about Captain Mac's horses. If the man from Freeport had arrived on schedule, he would have already loaded them into his trailer. She imagined Stormy's confusion as the strange man forced him aboard. The gray mustang would probably whinny and search for Alyssa's familiar scent. And as the days passed in a strange barn among strange people, maybe his heart would break. Alyssa felt a sharp lump rise in her throat at the thought that she would never see the horses again.

The shrimp boat veered to the right once again and chugged toward the ocean between the north and south rock jetties that stretched to the sea like opened arms. Alyssa couldn't believe her eyes. She let the dirty curtain fall back over the porthole, not wanting to look anymore. Nobody in his right mind would be going out to sea with a hurricane coming. Even though he would be heading up the coastline away from the storm, the ocean waves would be large and the rain might catch up with the boat. Besides, she didn't trust Berta or any other hurricane. They didn't always go where the weather forecasters expected them to go. They were one of the most unpredictable forces on earth. Only a drunkard with half a brain would be doing this.

Alyssa trembled all over, and her stomach churned. She thought she was going to throw up any minute. Then she saw Dylan looking scared and lost. She forced a smile and motioned for him to come over and sit beside her on the floor. She wrote him a note saying that they would go ashore as soon as Randon was asleep. She was glad Dylan didn't ask her how they were going to get ashore, because Alyssa wasn't sure herself. She had seen an emergency raft tied to the top of the pilothouse. If Randon fell into a deep sleep like Suzanne claimed he would, maybe Alyssa could talk Ty into letting her use the raft to get ashore.

Perhaps it wasn't the greatest plan in the world, but it was the best she could do. She gave Dylan a piece of chewing gum from her pocket and let him play with her slingshot. A little while later, he played a game of pick up sticks with Marie, and everyone seemed to relax a little.

Alyssa wished she could share their fun feelings, but the memory monster inside her—that gnawing, clawing animal—was trying to get free from its pen once again. The rocking boat, being below deck, hearing the wind whistle—all of these things were disturbing the monster. Alyssa tried to push the memory away. She fought it with all her willpower, but one thing kept crawling back: Her mother had died and her father had vanished three years ago in a boat caught in a storm. But Alyssa, a mere child of ten, had managed to escape. Why? Did her parents sacrifice themselves to save their daughter? Did the boat go down because of something Alyssa had done? Or was it just a freakish quirk of fate that she had been spared?

Alyssa couldn't shake the feeling that something was out there waiting for her. Something the Indians called *Urican*, the devil wind. It was more than whirling wind and water, it was a living creature with a will of its own. Alyssa could feel its cold arms opening wide, beckoning her. Three years ago she had slipped out of its watery embrace. Maybe this time she would not be so lucky.

Chapter Ten

DISCOVERED

Soon the smell of frying fish and potatoes drifted into the quarters below, making Alyssa's stomach even more queasy. Suzanne and Marie insisted she join them in the games, but Alyssa could not concentrate. All she could think about was how upset Aunt Melinda and Uncle Steven were going to be when they discovered that Dylan was missing. Captain Mac would probably get mad if he found her runaway note on the chest of drawers. They would think that she had taken Dylan with her on purpose. A feeling of helplessness filled her heart. She wished she could make a run for the top deck and jump into the ocean. But the waves were too rough and the shrimp boat was too far from the shore now. Besides, she was sure Dylan was a poor swimmer. More than likely, he was "allergic" to seawater, too.

Dishes clattered, then the door opened.

"Lunch is ready," Ty's mother shouted down at them. "You girls come fix yourselves a plate." She wiped beads of sweat from her forehead with the back of the hand holding a greasy spatula.

"Alyssa," she said in a lowered voice. "I reckon y'all better hide someplace till after Randon finishes eating. I don't think he'd be too happy to find you on board."

"We'll bring you something to eat in a minute," Suzanne whispered.

Alyssa had eaten only a tiny piece of birthday cake that morning, but she wasn't hungry. The girls hid Alyssa under the bedspread on the lower bunk and piled pillows on top of her until she could hardly breathe. They did the same to Dylan on the upper bunk. She heard plates clang, and then smelled food very close and knew that the girls had come back. She felt the mattress move as the girls sat down.

"Want some fish?" Marie whispered to Dylan.

"I'm really starving," he whispered back. "But don't you have something besides fish?"

"No. It's good. You'll like it," Marie said.

Alyssa imagined the turned-up nose and expression of repugnance on her brother's face. She was surprised to hear him say okay as he took the food.

"*Mmm* . . . this is good," Dylan's muffled voice said.

Alyssa smiled to herself. She knew that Dylan had always loved fish. She wished that Aunt Melinda were there to see him eating it. Alyssa chuckled to herself at the thought of her aunt's expression. She wondered if it was safe for her to lift the bedspread from her face yet. It was getting very hot and hard to breathe. Suddenly she heard heavy footsteps coming closer.

"Ty, steer for a while and keep an eye on things," a man's gruff voice said.

"Be real quiet," Suzanne whispered. "Randon's coming down to use the head."

The floor creaked with the man's heavy footfall, then the bathroom door slammed shut. In a minute the door opened again. The smell of beer drifted under the covers into Alyssa's nostrils. She heard the man's heavy breathing over her head.

"Well now, girls, that fish looks mighty good. At least your mama's good for something around here." He snorted then broke into rollicking laughter.

A layer of sweat covered Alyssa's body, and she fought for air. Ever so slightly she moved her fingers to make a little opening in the bedspread near her face, but the air was hot and still. Alyssa had not liked being confined in tight spaces such as closets, or caves, or under bedcovers since the storm three years ago. She preferred lots of air and open space.

She knew there was more to her fear than just hating tight places. Something worse. Her heart pounded faster and her head whirred as memories tried to push their way to the surface. She didn't want to remember—not here, not now. But as the boat pitched and the wind whistled past the portholes and the air grew thinner, suddenly a memory broke free from its cage and roared in her face:

I was hiding below deck in Father's charter boat the day it went down.

The truth hit Alyssa like a rock between the eyes. Of course, her parents would not have allowed her to be on board in a tropical storm. How could anyone have ever thought that?

Alyssa and her mother had planned to shop for school clothes that day, but the storm canceled their plans. It was a tropical storm, not a full-fledged hurricane, so most islanders had stayed. And many stores had remained open.

Alyssa had wanted to go shopping; she whined and complained, and her mother grew impatient. Then something happened. What was it? It was a radio signal on Channel 16—an emergency at sea. Alyssa's father had already secured his charter boat. He had no reason to go back out to sea. But some tourists were caught in their small yacht with a failing motor. The Coast Guard cutters and smaller rescue boats were busy helping a stranded oil derrick crew. So Alyssa's father decided to help the yacht since he was closer than anyone else.

Alyssa's father was a great sailor, but the charter boat had a new motor in it that hadn't been tested in stormy weather. Her mother decided to go with him. Alyssa was mad the shopping trip had been canceled and even angrier when they told her she could not go with them.

"No, Alyssa, you and Dylan have to stay with Captain Mac," her mother had said as she slipped into her rain slicker. "It's too dangerous for you out there. Keep Dylan company so he won't be afraid of the storm."

But Alyssa was a stubborn, dreamy child who wanted to witness a rescue at sea. She wanted to feel the wind and rain in her face and the thrill of being tossed from side to side in a great storm.

She had heard so many tall tales from her grandfather and Uncle D about those wild, wonderful days when they were young and had sailed the roughest waters in the world. She wanted to embrace that devil wind and feel its kiss.

So she sneaked out of Captain Mac's shack and headed down to the charter boat while her parents were gathering up ropes and dry blankets and medical supplies. Then she hid below, under the bedcovers. But it hadn't been fun at all. The waves punched the boat with angry fists of water, and she felt sick and threw up. Her father had been furious when he found her on board, but it was too late by then. Her mother didn't chastise her. She just held her close as the boat engine began to sputter. Alyssa's heart had never pounded so fast, and she wanted to throw up again, but there was nothing left in her stomach except bitter bile.

The sound of coughing suddenly jerked Alyssa away from her memory. She was glad. She didn't think she could stand to relive what had happened next. Quickly her brain pushed the memory beast back down into its cage. At least for a while.

Alyssa didn't realize that she was sniffing and whimpering softly, until Marie whispered, "Are you all right, Alyssa?"

Alyssa took a deep breath, stuck her hand out of the covers, and gave the okay signal.

"Who are you talking to, gal?" Randon asked in a loud voice from near the door.

"Nobody," Marie replied. "Me and Suzanne are just playing cards."

"Bring me that whiskey bottle I keep stashed under the cabinet."

Alyssa felt Suzanne's body stiffen, and Marie made a small whimper.

"Randon, honey, now don't be drinking in the broad daylight. You ain't touched your food yet," Ty's mother whined from the stairway. "Don't you have to be alert to take the boat through this weather? What if—"

A loud pop cut her voice short. Alyssa began to tremble.

"Can't none of you ever do one thing you're told to? Why are all of you against me?"

He bumped into something. A volcano of foul language erupted from his lips.

"I said fetch that bottle," he demanded. "Just once in my life I wish somebody would do what I said. Between you and the gov'ment and their stupid rules, a man can't hardly make a living anymore. First they let those Vietnamese come in and take all our shrimp, then they make us put on stupid T.E.D. contraptions to save the turtles. *Turtles!* What about saving humans? Ain't people more important than *turtles?* And those stinking foreigners . . . they ain't normal, working day and night like they do."

Alyssa mentally pictured the man that she hadn't seen yet. He would be tall and large, towering over the delicate girls. He would probably have his hands on his hips and a scowl on his face.

The coughing came again, this time louder and uncontrollable. The first time Alyssa had heard it, she thought it was Suzanne or Marie. Now she realized it was coming from Dylan in the upper bunk.

"What the . . . ?"

Alyssa heard Randon jerk the covers from the upper berth. Suddenly a hand yanked back her own thin bedspread and fresh air gushed over her hot, sweaty body. She sat up and stared into a pair of chilly black eyes set in a ruddy face fringed with a patchy black beard and a drooping mustache. He wasn't nearly as tall as she had imagined. His belly pushed out against his undershirt and hung down over his belt.

"What in tarnation is going on here!"

Alyssa swallowed hard as she scooted to the back of the bunk bed. She squished her body into the far corner against the wall, where it would be harder for Randon to take a swing at her.

Suzanne leapt up and stood between Alyssa and her stepfather.

"These are my friends," she said. "We were playing a game when you started the boat up. We didn't know you were going to Louisiana."

"What's your name, gal?" he asked Alyssa.

Alyssa opened her mouth, but an ugly squeak was all that came out.

"She can't talk, Randon," Ty's mother said. "She's mute. And this is her little brother."

By now Dylan was wheezing and coughing. Ty's mother helped him down from the bed, then led him upstairs. She gave him a drink of water. He stopped coughing but went into a bad case of hiccups.

"Well, that's great, just great!" Randon roared as he watched Dylan. "Now I'm gonna have to either turn around and go back toward a hurricane or get accused of kidnapping a sick boy and a mental retardee."

Alyssa gritted her teeth, scooted off the bed, and stood up. One foot was asleep and tingly, but she didn't care. She ran for the door, flying up the steps before Randon could grab her.

Dylan stood in the pilothouse next to Ty's

mother. Alyssa grabbed his hand, then rushed to the side of the boat and leaned over the gunwale.

The dark green waters swished as the prow slowly cut through the whitecaps. The wind whipped the foam from the caps and threw salty mist into Alyssa's face. As she pulled Dylan close and placed her hands on his shoulders, she felt him trembling. She knew that he was looking at the shoreline and that he must be thinking, as she was, that it was too far and too hopeless.

Chapter Eleven

A CRY

FOR

HELP

The salty air sprayed Alyssa's hot face and lifted her limp hair as it had done a thousand times when she stood on the beach looking toward the ocean. No matter how bad the weather or how cruel the season, she had never hated the sea. Even after her mother had drowned and her father had vanished, she could not hold her loss against the sea. The storm was a separate force, something that only used the ocean's back to travel upon to reach its destination. Surely the sea hated the devil wind swirling along its spine. Perhaps the waves radiating out from the eye of the storm were great chill bumps as the ocean shivered in repulsion.

But when Alyssa saw the shoreline so far away and the menacing gray sky, for the first time she felt bitterness toward the waters that separated her and Dylan from their home. The water here seemed to be a different color, the air seemed to hold a different scent, and even the wind felt strange. It was the sea, but it wasn't *her* sea. And she did not trust it.

After standing at the rail for several minutes, Alyssa heard a squeaking noise accompanied by the sound of a motor. When she turned, she saw Ty. His knee-high rubber boots glistened as he stood near a pile of squirming shrimp and fish that had just been dumped from a net.

"What happened?" he asked as he ducked under the steel cable of the winch. "Did Randon hit you?"

Alyssa shook her head and pointed to the distant shore.

Ty sighed. He lifted the brim of the cap that half hid his face. "I'm sorry this happened. As soon as we get back to land, I'll buy you a bus ticket back to Galveston. I know you didn't want to come along. I'm really sorry. I told you I'm the unluckiest guy in the world." He seized a short-handled shovel and scooped up a pile of shrimp.

Alyssa's heart ached for him. She wanted to tell him that she didn't blame him; it wasn't his fault. She tapped his shoulder and gave him a little salute. It was all she could think of. Slowly a crooked grin came to Ty's lips, then he nodded.

"You're okay, Blondie," he said. "But if y'all are gonna stay topside, you'd better put your rain slickers back on. I don't think we can outrun the storm. Randon's making me do a little trawling as we go. He thinks there might be some white shrimp along here."

The sound of heavy footsteps and a loud voice made them turn around.

"I don't allow no idle hands on this boat, little gal. As long as you and your brother are getting a free ride, you'd better help out. Get that bucket and start bailing out some of that bilge water from the engine room. The dern pump has been sputtering off and on."

He tossed a pail at Alyssa and she caught it with a grunt. Then he pushed Dylan toward the engine room. Dylan's face turned pale as he looked down into the stinky, dirty water. Alyssa knew that Dylan would start coughing again, so she gently pushed him aside and began dipping the bucket as fast as she could.

Alyssa balanced herself at the small engine compartment, one foot in the shallow water and the other foot on the deck. The burning oil and diesel fumes and the loud sound of the popping motor soon made her head ache. Randon stood over her a moment longer, complaining about her work, then walked over to Ty and examined the pile of shrimp.

"Looks okay. There's a good mix of white shrimp in there. Let's go ahead and lower the main nets."

"The waters are pretty rough," Ty said. "I'm not a very good rigger. Maybe we'd better wait till Johnny comes back. I might mess up the nets."

"I told you I fired Johnny yesterday. I got fed up with his smart mouth," Randon said. "Besides, it's about time you learned how to be a rigger anyhow."

"Whatever you say, Randon," Ty muttered, and climbed over ice chests and cables to the winch controls. He removed the triangular metal stabilizers from the large black overhead outriggers, which were now opened wide like the arms of a skeleton. Randon freed the heavy wooden paddles at the tip of each outrigger. For a moment they swayed precariously, almost banging against the side of the boat.

Ty and Randon lay the massive nets on the deck, then carefully tied the bags and tested the knot. Randon returned to the pilothouse and slowed the motor. Then he gave Ty the signal. Ty groaned as he shoved the heavy nets over the rail and they disappeared into the green waters. With a shout from Ty, Randon increased the engine speed and the winch lowered the swinging doors slowly after the nets. Randon put the boat on automatic pilot and returned to look over the gunwales.

"Now, boy, you watch them nets real careful." He stumbled over the shovel, cursed, and staggered to the cabin, where he plopped down in the pilot's seat again.

Alyssa bailed water, keeping a watchful eye on Dylan, who sat quietly nearby. Less than an hour later Randon shouted to Ty: "Bring 'em up! I'm too tired to steer anymore. My head's about to split wide open. We'll trawl again after I've had a little nap."

Ty turned the winch lever. The motor and cables creaked, and soon the heavy nets rose to the surface. Ty positioned the boom over the deck, then jerked the rope around the nets. Thousands of shiny shrimp and other sea life showered onto the deck. Randon returned to the cabin, where he turned off the engine, then stretched out on the homemade bench.

"Wake me when you're finished with that catch," he mumbled, then rolled on his side.

"Alyssa, Dylan, wanna help me with this?" Ty called out. Alyssa was glad to stop bailing for a while, and Dylan welcomed the change.

The pink shrimp glistened and wiggled on the deck. A few fish flopped about, and crabs scrambled toward the dark corners as the boat rocked from side to side. Some eels and jellyfish wiggled in the nets.

Suzanne and Marie joined Alyssa and Dylan and showed them how to sort the shrimp according to size. They tossed the fish back overboard, except for a few they placed in a bucket of seawater. The sea gulls that had been following for miles screamed and dived for the discards.

"Put the jumbo shrimp in this pile," Ty explained. "Medium go here and the little ones over there. Open season started today, so we can trawl with any size net we want." He tossed pairs of gloves to all the girls. "Who wants to head the shrimp?" he asked. Both of his sisters frowned and shook their heads, so he sighed. "Guess that leaves it to me. Oh well, I'm used to it." He sat on a short stool, hunched over the piles of shrimp, and began breaking the heads off.

"Curly, you and Marie can scoot those baby crabs over the side. They're too little for anything." Marie got a broom and showed Dylan how to scare the crabs toward holes in the side of the boat. Alyssa felt a wave of pride when she saw her brother working without complaining. He hardly seemed like the same little boy who had been biting his fingernails earlier that day.

For a long time Alyssa stooped over the piles of shrimp. Their long, delicate feelers tickled and their sharp beaks pricked her fingers, even through the gloves. Hundreds of beady black eyes stared at her before the creatures met their fate. A dull ache started at the bottom of her back and spread upward until she didn't think she could stand another minute. The job didn't seem to bother Ty. When they had finished, he packed the shrimp in large containers of ice.

"Randon's in a deep sleep," he whispered to Alyssa. "I'm going to try to get us real close to shore, so you and Dylan can get off. If you don't mind, you need to bail the bilge water a little while longer." He stepped up to the pilot's cabin and started the engine.

A few minutes later, Alyssa saw a boat adrift off the port side and heard voices yelling.

"It's a shrimp boat," Ty said, squinting and leaning over the wheel. "I think it's stalled out. I can't understand anything they're saying. Must be Vietnamese." Ty flipped on the CB radio. He spoke into the mouthpiece, but no one responded.

"Ahoy!" Ty shouted after he'd shut off the engine and walked to the rail. "Are you in trouble?"

"Yes, we have trouble," a man called back in a heavy Vietnamese accent. "Engine broke. Need fuel line."

"Did you call for help?"

Several voices replied at the same time. "Radio broke."

"I'll call in some help for you," Ty yelled. But before he could turn around, a large, tanned hand grabbed his shoulder and jerked him back from the rail.

"No you won't," Randon said as he pushed Ty aside. "Let those leeches get their own help. If it wasn't for them breeding all over the place, I'd be making a decent living."

"But . . . their radio's down, too. If that hurricane changes course and comes this way, they'll capsize or they might run aground if they drift ashore."

"Good! The fewer of them, the better for us."

"But, Randon, all they need is a piece of fuel

line. We've got some extra below. I could pull up real close and toss it over to them."

For a reply Randon struck Ty across the ear.

"Shut up! I'm the boss here. Get them nets untangled. And forget about dropping 'em again. We don't have time for more trawling today. It's getting too rough."

Randon cupped his hands over his mouth and shouted across the choppy sea.

"Sorry, no radio here. No fuel line. No helpy." He chuckled.

The Vietnamese shrimpers whispered and argued among themselves. As Randon started the engine, the men shouted again excitedly and pleaded for help. Randon spit out a string of curses.

"Go back where you came from," he called. "We don't want you here." He jerked the steering wheel around and gave the engine full throttle. The wake of Randon's trawler rocked the stranded shrimp boat. Ty ran to the pilothouse and pulled at the wheel.

"You can't abandon them!"

The strike from the back of Randon's hand knocked Ty to his knees.

"Lucille, come take the wheel while I teach this spoiled brat son of yours a lesson." He grabbed Ty's arm and dragged him below.

The screaming and yelling below brought Dylan to Alyssa's side. His sad brown eyes filled with tears as he stared at the closed door.

"He's beating Ty, isn't he?" he said between sniffs. Alyssa felt helpless. She pulled her brother close and wrapped her arms around his skinny shoulders. It was raining lightly now, so she helped Dylan into the slicker that Marie had brought up from below, and then put hers on, too.

Randon soon returned topside, slamming the door behind him. "Don't come out till I say you can!" he shouted. He spat over the gunwale, then turned to the others huddled together.

"Well, what are you staring at?" he demanded. "You get back to hauling bilge water." He pointed to Alyssa. "And you gals finish cleaning up the deck. And *you*"—he pointed a short, plump finger at Dylan—"you're about the most useless skinny-bones I've ever seen. Can't lift a bucket or cull shrimp worth a hoot. Maybe I should just throw you overboard to the sharks." He burst into laughter when he saw Dylan turn pale and stumble backward.

"Oh, do you want your mommy?"

Anger ripped through Alyssa. She knew Dylan wasn't the strongest boy in the world and he had a lot of faults, but he was sweet in a way. And besides, Dylan was her brother. She wasn't going to let anyone bully him around.

Alyssa gently pushed Dylan behind her out of the way, then lifted a bucket of bilge water. With all her strength, she sloshed the dirty, smelly liquid into Randon's face.

He screamed and pawed at his eyes, then charged at her. She tried to run, but she slipped on the slimy water and fell at Randon's feet. Helplessly she watched the big man lift Dylan into the air.

"I think I'll feed you to the sharks," he said with a laugh. The burly man steadied his legs on the rolling deck and pretended he was going to toss Dylan overboard. Dylan screamed and flailed, but that only made Randon squeeze him harder.

As Alyssa struggled to her feet, she saw a shovel go high into the air, then heard the crack as it came down on top of Randon's head. He groaned, dropped Dylan to the deck, then collapsed with a heavy thud.

Chapter Twelve

INTO

THE

SEA

Maybe Alyssa should have felt bad to see a man sprawled motionless on the deck. But all she could think of was the way he had treated Ty and Ty's mother and Dylan. Maybe he didn't deserve what he got, but at the moment all Alyssa felt was relief and gratitude to Ty's mother, who stood above him, the shovel still in her trembling hands.

Everyone was dazed. Only the sound of the wind and the waves sloshing against the prow broke the silence. The sea gulls that followed the boat, screaming and diving for discarded shrimp heads or fish, circled overhead or landed on the mast and outriggers like a curious crowd of spectators.

"Momma, is he dead?" Marie's tiny voice rang out like a clear bell, rousing them out of their stupor. Ty's mother didn't reply. She stood in the same place, clutching the shovel, staring at her husband. She didn't blink or move or even seem to be alive.

Ty, who had come up from below at the sound of the commotion, squatted beside Randon. He pressed his finger on the man's thick bull neck.

"He ain't dead," he said without emotion. He gently removed the shovel from his mother's hands. "We'd better go back to Galveston and get him to a doctor, Momma."

"I only married him to keep the family together," the woman said in a weak, thin voice. "But maybe you'd all been better off in foster homes. I should've never married him." She repeated the words over and over and didn't move.

Ty's sisters rushed to their mother and wrapped their arms around her waist. Ty rolled Randon over onto his back. A spot of red stained the deck beneath his head.

"Help me get him to the cabin," Ty said. It took nearly all of them fighting the heavy man's weight and the pitch and roll of the boat, but finally they lifted him onto the padded bench. Randon groaned a few times, then breathed heavily and began snoring.

"I think he's sleeping it off," Ty said to his mother. "He'll probably just wake up with a headache in the morning and not even remember what happened. Don't worry, Momma. If he asks any questions, I'll say that it was me who hit him. You hear that, girls?" The girls nodded solemnly. Their mother sat on the edge of the bed and stared down at her husband in silence.

"I'm turning the boat around and going back to Galveston," Ty called down to Alyssa from the pilothouse as he took the engine off automatic pilot and turned the wheel.

"But there's a hurricane coming, isn't there?" Suzanne said as she climbed up next to her brother.

"We'll dock before it hits. We still have time to get up the channel some." He gave the engine full throttle and ripped through the water.

About thirty minutes later, they saw the stranded Vietnamese boat again. The men aboard waved their arms and shouted for help.

"Alyssa, take the wheel a minute," Ty said. "I'm going to get some fuel line for those people."

While Alyssa held the wheel steady, Ty crawled into the engine room with a flashlight and came out a few minutes later holding several feet of line. He had a strange expression on his pale face as he took back the wheel and slowed the engine.

"Alyssa, go back to the engine room and start bailing out water as fast as you can," he whispered. "That pump is only half working. Get Suzanne to help you. Hurry!"

Alyssa found an extra bucket and handed it to Suzanne. As Alyssa stepped inside the small room, stinking, murky water rose above her shins. The girls decided a relay system would be the fastest way to bail. Alyssa filled a bucket, then handed it up to Suzanne. While Suzanne tossed the water overboard, Alyssa filled the second bucket. They worked fast, but they could not seem to lower the water level in the room.

Alyssa felt the boat slowing and saw that Ty had pulled alongside the stranded Vietnamese shrimp boat. The choppy waters rocked them precariously, and the low, thick clouds threatened as the first band of the hurricane's outer swirling mass approached. To the west, over Galveston Island, the clouds hovered even thicker and darker. Alyssa knew that the first heavy rains would reach them soon. Already a light rain was falling from the dark sky, and the air had turned so cool that chill bumps rose along her arms under her raincoat.

Ty brought his boat as close as possible, then tossed the piece of fuel line over to the Vietnamese men. They waved and cheered and thanked him profusely.

When a large wave lifted the shrimp boat, then dropped it hard, a flash of memory burst into Alyssa's head without warning. That day in the charter boat three years ago, her mother had been rocking her in her arms, telling her it wasn't her fault, that everything would be all right. She told Alyssa to sit on the bed for a moment while she crossed the room to get some nylon ropes needed to rescue the yacht in peril. Then a heavy wave had tossed the charter boat and rolled it to one side.

Alyssa fought back the memory. In her heart, she knew something terrible happened next. She tried to concentrate on the bailing by watching Suzanne's slender arms. They heaved the buckets as fast as they could, but they were not gaining any ground. The pump sputtered constantly. Each time they got the water to a safe level to keep it out of the engine and thought they might rest, another wave of seawater would spew over the stern of the boat. The waves were monstrously high swells now, and the wind grew stronger as they came closer to the island and the hurricane. A deep gloom had settled over the ocean, making it almost as dark as night.

The first storm band hit with a roar. The rain fell in cold, slanted bullets, thumping the wooden deck like muffled machine-gun fire. Suzanne screamed just as a peal of thunder and bolt of lightning rocked the dark sky. She jumped into the engine room beside Alyssa.

"Momma, we need help!" Suzanne shouted across the deck. "Get another bucket!"

But her mother didn't move. She sat on the edge of the bed, tears in her red, swollen eyes as she stared at Randon's sleeping form.

"What's wrong?" Ty called from the pilot-house.

"We're taking on too much water. The pump's a-fixing to go out on us. Head for shore, Ty. Hurry!" Suzanne shrieked.

Ty turned to them, his pale face haloed by the yellow glow from the overhead light in the cabin. His worried blue eyes searched each face, then came to rest on the two smallest children huddled on the steps leading below.

"Marie, Curly, come here and hold the wheel."

The two children looked at each other, then got up.

"I . . . I don't know how . . . I can't do it," Dylan began, but Ty patted his back.

"Sure, you can do it. Each of you take one side of the wheel. Just hold it steady, no matter what. I know you can do it, Curly. You've got strong muscles." Ty squeezed Dylan's skinny arm, then grinned. Alyssa felt sick inside knowing that their fate was in the hands of small children. But her heart was bursting with pride in her brother for being brave. He took his side of the wheel, staring ahead gravely. His was not the face of Alyssa's eight-year-old brother but the face of her father.

Ty rushed to the engine room and pulled Suzanne and Alyssa out. He grabbed a bucket and bailed like a frenzied maniac. The two girls emptied the buckets as fast as they could. Rain pelted Alyssa's rain slicker and plastered her hair in her eyes. Sometimes the boat pitched and rolled so hard, they had to hold onto the winch cables, or nets, or anything they could find. And during that time, Ty kept screaming for more buckets.

They worked frantically for several minutes before a wave, bigger than all the previous ones, rolled over them, knocking the girls to the deck. With a shutter and creak, the pump shut off. No matter how hard Ty tried, cussing and kicking, the pump would not start again.

"Ty, come help us!" Marie's shrill voice sang out. Ty looked toward the cabin, where the children clung to the wheel. With a curse, he dropped the bucket and hurried back to the pilothouse. He picked up the CB radio mouthpiece and called "Mayday" again and again through thick static.

Alyssa's muscles ached and her shoulders felt as if her arms were being jerked from their sockets. Suzanne, too, groaned with each bucket she hauled. They both knew it was only a matter of minutes until the engine would flood. In the distance Alyssa thought she saw pale yellow lights outlining a shore. A brilliant bolt of lightning ripped through the sky, revealing land. She prayed it was Galveston Island. If they could just hang on a little longer, they could make it ashore.

Suddenly a wall of water lifted them high, then savagely rolled the boat to one side. Water flooded into the engine room, and the motor hissed and stopped. Suzanne held tightly to Alyssa's hand until the boat righted itself. It was pointless to bail water now, so they tossed their buckets aside and crawled to the cabin.

"Help me get the life raft!" Ty shouted over the whistling wind.

Marie had found a flashlight below. She shone it on the life-raft rope while Ty unfastened the rubber pack and pulled the cord. With a hiss, the raft inflated and covered the prow of the deck. He secured its line to the rail with a slipknot.

"Momma!" Ty said, shaking his mother. "Momma! We're gonna abandon the ship. It's taking on too much water. Let's get Randon inside the raft."

The woman stared blankly into Ty's face. Slowly she rose. Everyone except her groaned and grunted as they pulled Randon into a sitting position. He opened his eyes. One hand went to the back of his head, and he moaned.

"What . . . ," he muttered.

"Get into the raft," Ty instructed the man as he helped him stand up. Randon's knees buckled two times, but finally he was sitting in the raft, a dazed expression on his confused face.

"I don't have enough life preservers for everybody," Ty said as he fastened a big orange jacket around the two smallest children, then slipped a flotation ring around Randon. He gave another jacket to his mother and held the last one in his hand.

"We'll share it," Suzanne said as she slid one arm through the left armhole and put Alyssa's into the right hole. Ty was the only person who didn't have a life preserver of any kind, but he didn't seem to care. He gave Suzanne and Alyssa each a fiberglass paddle.

Ty stood on the deck beside the life-raft rope that was still secured to the cabin.

"I think the Coast Guard got my message," he said. "They'll probably be here before the boat sinks. But we'll be ready just in case."

But the Coast Guard did not come. The boat rocked and everyone knew it was too late. Each new wave brought more water over the sides and stern. Already the hold below deck was filling up. The ice chests full of shrimp had washed overboard, along with everything else loose on the deck. The only things left were the life raft and its cargo of people.

"Hold on!" Ty shouted as he quickly jerked the slipknot free and leapt into the raft beside Alyssa. She saw the mountain of water just as he grabbed the loop next to her. Alyssa closed her eyes and gritted her teeth as the water lifted the raft and flung it into the sea. Suzanne's fingers dug into Alyssa's arm, and Marie's voice screeched in her ear.

For a moment Alyssa didn't know if she was in the raft or in the ocean. All she felt was cold water surrounding her, and all she could hear was the sound of her heart pounding in her chest. She held her breath and waited. When she first opened her eyes, she saw only darkness. Then she turned around. About two miles away the shoreline lights dimly twinkled. Everyone was all right, even Randon, who was just coming out of his stupor.

"What's happening?" the man whined as he rolled his eyes from side to side and spat out a stream of seawater.

"Let me do the talking," Ty whispered to his mother. "Randon, you fell and hit your head on the gunwale. The storm's hitting us something fierce right now. The bilge pump broke, then the engine flooded. The shrimp boat's sinking. We had to get into the life raft. But the shore's not too far away."

"Dern fools . . . ," Randon started to shout, but stopped with a grimace as he put one hand on his head.

"Let's paddle toward shore," Ty said.

Even though her arms were stiff and sore from bailing, Alyssa began pushing the oar through the rough water.

She wasn't sure how long they had been paddling, but they didn't seem to be getting any closer to shore. The first storm band had passed over, and now it was light again. Only thin clouds swirled above, and the rain was very soft.

"Is the storm over?" Dylan asked Ty in a timid voice.

Ty scratched his head and shrugged. "It doesn't seem possible. But I've never been out on the ocean during a hurricane. I suppose this is just the beginning of it."

Alyssa wanted to tell him how right he was. The first band of clouds was nothing compared to the next and the next. Each one would be stronger and last longer, until finally the storm wall itself passed over. Inside that boiling fury of wind and water, the heart of the devil wind beat. Winds would slam at up to 120 miles an hour, maybe more, and rain would pound the earth, turning streams into rivers, and rivers into oceans. And the sea would swallow up the land.

Alyssa felt a stinging pain in her hands and looked down. The paddle had rubbed big blisters on her palms and fingers. Some had already burst and were oozing blood, but the coldness was numbing them. She glanced around the raft. Dylan and Marie huddled together under a raincoat that belonged to Randon. Randon was still groggy, and Ty's mother stared blankly ahead.

Alyssa was frightened by the storm, but there was something else bothering her. Everything felt like a dream—almost as if she were watching herself in a home movie. The raft rising and falling with the sea, her aching arms and tired body, the salt water in her eyes and mouth and hair—everything felt familiar. She had seen the tip of the shrimp boat's prow sinking. Bubbles gurgled, then the last of the air had jetted out with a swoosh as the sea had devoured it. Now she could see the shore in the distance.

The same thing had happened to her three years before. Now that crazy, suppressed memory threatened to take over her mind. She was scared of the water and the wind and being on the sea, but the thought of remembering what happened that other time was more frightening than all of Berta's fury.

Alyssa fought against the memory, until finally the monster calmed and left her alone. She tricked the beast by allowing herself one small memory— being on the raft, exhausted, and finally being rescued and taken ashore. She remembered all those details clearly now. But she refused to let that final terrible memory rear its head.

"Look, there's a boat out there!" It was Dylan who saw the blinking red lights first. Everyone turned in the direction that his tiny finger pointed. As if given a signal, everyone in the raft shouted and waved their hands. Even Randon's deep voice bellowed like a scared bull's.

Ty flicked the flashlight off and on as he waved his rain hat. Finally the distant boat flicked its lights and hooted its horn.

Everyone cheered, and relief swept over Alyssa's weary body. She put the paddle down and watched the boat draw closer. After several minutes, she heard men's voices. They spoke Vietnamese.

Randon cursed under his breath when he recognized the shrimp boat that he had abandoned earlier in the day.

"Shoot! I know they ain't gonna help us," Randon hissed. "The lousy foreign scum."

"After the way you treated them, I wouldn't blame them one bit for leaving us out here," Ty said.

Suzanne heaved a heavy sigh and Alyssa guessed they were both thinking the same thing. If Randon weren't on the raft, their chances of being rescued would be much better. They all waited on needles and pins as the shrimpers pulled up closer. It was turning dark again, and the wind and rain were getting stronger. The next storm band was approaching. If they didn't get aboard the shrimp boat within the next few minutes, they would be doomed to fight the sea on the flimsy raft.

Alyssa held her breath as she watched the faces of the men above. The tables were turned now, and they were the ones who held the fate of Randon's family in their hands. Alyssa prayed that they would show more kindness than Randon had shown them.

Chapter Thirteen

AMAZING

GRACE

Van was the name of the man who owned the shrimp boat. When he recognized Randon, it seemed like forever to Alyssa before he turned to his companions and spoke. They talked excitedly. One stomped away angrily. But another pointed to Ty and grinned.

The men lowered a heavy rope with a knot tied on its end. One by one, they hauled up the passengers of the life raft, starting with the smallest children. They saved Randon for last, and Alyssa thought she knew what was in everyone's mind as the small men struggled to lift Randon's bearlike hulk over the rail. Alyssa was surprised when Randon thanked the men and shook their hands in what seemed like genuine gratitude. He even helped them bring up the raft and secure it to the top of the pilot's cabin.

Alyssa was nearly soaked to the bone in spite of the raincoat. She shivered uncontrollably until one of the men covered her with a flimsy flowered bedspread. The shrimp boat was a small, thirty-foot bay boat that had no quarters below. The girls, Dylan, and Ty's mother crowded into the cabin as best as they could while the men stayed on deck.

The second squall still raged overhead, dropping buckets of rain, but the lightning and thunder were not as violent as before. Even though the fuel line had been repaired, Van's engine still sputtered. Randon squeezed his big body into the engine room and worked on the motor while Van shone the flashlight on the equipment. Everyone was surprised that Randon was helping, but Alyssa remembered that Uncle D always told her that storms at sea make friends out of the most unlikely men.

Alyssa didn't know exactly what time it was. Her wristwatch had stopped working long ago. It was dark and the streetlights on the island had flickered on even though it was not nighttime yet.

The children were exhausted, especially Dylan. Alyssa let him lay his head on her lap while she sat on the cabin floor and leaned against the wall. Ty's mother sat beside her, and her daughters curled up next to her, looking sick. Alyssa wasn't sure how she could even think of sleeping in such weather, but soon her eyelids grew heavy and she could no longer fight off sleep.

It was a fitful sleep. She dreamed of her grandfather's horses in the old days when her father had been a child. She knew it was her father in the dream, even though the boy looked amazingly like Dylan with his black-rimmed glasses, sitting in Lana Turner's lap, smiling and waving. Alyssa ran after the horse, and though she was afoot, somehow she caught up. But when the boy on the horse turned around, it wasn't her father or Dylan. It was Ty.

"Blondie, wake up."

Alyssa opened her eyes and stared into Ty's face. It dripped with rain. A pale gray streak of light showed overhead and the rain had slackened. Off to their right Bolivar Peninsula jutted out into the sea; to the left, Galveston Island beckoned. But between the boat and the safety of the channel, rock jetties stuck out from the ends of both strips of land. The storm surge had raised the water level precariously close to the tops of the huge chunks of granite. Giant rolling waves crashed savagely over them, and the water churned white. To avoid the jetties, Van had to take the boat back out toward the sea about four miles, then turn in again. It was slow, rough going, but finally he reached the channel with its partly protected waters. The jetties and tip of Galveston Island blocked the largest waves, but the water was still very rough due to the stiff easterly wind.

Alyssa gently removed Dylan from her lap and stood. Out on the deck she leaned on the gunwale, bracing her body against the wind. She heard the bells of the buoys clanging wildly a few yards ahead. One had a green light, the other a red light. Along the main island she saw flashing yellow lights moving cautiously down Seawall Boulevard. She wondered if it could be a rescue team searching for Dylan and her at that very moment.

Guilt jabbed her heart when she thought about her grandfather and her aunt and uncle returning to the stables to find Dylan gone. They would be sick with worry about him. She wondered what was going through their minds. Did they think he had been kidnapped? Or had they found the runaway note on the chest of drawers and concluded that she had forced Dylan to go with her?

Panic flooded over Alyssa at the thought. She spun around and bumped into Ty. She pointed to Galveston, looming off the port side of the boat.

Ty cocked his head. For a moment his eyes followed the distant flashing lights of the vehicle.

"I know you want to go ashore, Blondie. But how? Van said he's taking the boat up the channel. If we're lucky we'll make it before the worst of the storm hits. I have a feeling that's going to be pretty soon." He glanced at the dark sky and shivered.

Alyssa wanted to tell him they still had a little time left. The next band of heavy rain would come soon, but it would be bearable. After that the wind and rain would gradually increase until it was continuous with no lulls and gusts. If they could get ashore and flag down a ride, they could be back at her grandfather's house before the storm pounded them.

As the shrimp boat chugged closer to the shore, Alyssa thought about the horses. Poor Stormy and Oscar and Jo-Jo and all the others. If the man from Freeport had not come to buy them, they might still be in the corral or in the stables. They would be trapped on low ground. The storm surge might sweep them across the island into the bay and to a sure death.

While pointing to the island with one hand, Alyssa grunted and slapped the gunwale over and over with the other. She swung one leg over the top as if she were going to leap overboard.

"Whoa, Blondie. Are you crazy?" Ty grabbed her waist and pulled her back. "Look at those waves. This is a hurricane, girl. It's safer for us to go with Van up the river."

Alyssa shook her head like a wild woman, making her wet hair fly from side to side. She whimpered, grunted, and pounded the rail until her hands throbbed and bled again.

"What are you so worried about? We'll be safe."

Alyssa fought back tears of frustration as she tried once again to make him understand. She made motions like a running horse. When his face remained blank, she went wild and slapped his chest. He caught her hands in his own and stared into her eyes.

"Horses? Is that it? You're worried about the horses?"

Alyssa sighed and nodded.

"Wait a second." Ty disappeared for a minute, then returned with Van.

"Van says he can take us a little closer to the shore, then we can lower the life raft. The east wind should carry you right to the tip end of the island. About a hundred yards or so." Ty paused. "Do you think you can handle it?"

Alyssa was moved with affection for Ty. She hugged his sturdy shoulders and placed a quick kiss on his wet face, then helped the men retrieve the raft from the wheelhouse.

"Where're you going?" a small voice asked as Alyssa slipped on a life jacket.

Alyssa turned around. Dylan stood behind her, a worried expression on his face.

"Alyssa, don't leave me. You're supposed to be looking after me, remember?" His pale face looked as gray as the sky above and his sad eyes glistened. Alyssa nodded and slid a jacket over his head and fastened it.

"You're crazy, but I can't let you two go alone," Ty said. He helped the men lower the lifeboat over the side by its long towrope. Alyssa, Dylan, then Ty climbed over the side of the rocking boat into the raft below.

"Ty DuVal! What in tarnation are you doing?" Randon's bull voice roared. He leaned over the gunwale, his big belly hanging like a sack of jelly.

"I'm going to make sure these two get home safe. I'll meet you and Momma at the rent-house after the storm is over."

The big man snorted. "Dern fool!" he muttered, then waved his hand as if swatting a fly.

As the men above released the rope, Alyssa looked up and saw Ty's mother and sisters lined against the gunwale. They waved and shouted. Tears streamed down their faces as if they would never see Ty again. She prayed they were wrong.

As Ty and Alyssa paddled away from the shrimp boat, a wave lifted them high and dropped them with a slap. It occurred to Alyssa that maybe she was making a mistake. But it was too late now. She paddled for her life with the frenzy of a madman. The waves threw fistfuls of foam into her face, stinging her eyes with salty brine. Ty shrieked out instructions behind her, but they had little control over the raft. The waves shook the fragile craft and turned it sideways, then straightened it out again. Alyssa's arms, still sore from bailing water, soon felt as if someone had pulled them from their sockets. Her eyes burned and felt swollen. It was an effort just to keep them open.

At last they saw the shallow, sandy area near Big Reef at the tip of the island. The life raft rocked over the sand now covered by the ocean. The powerful east wind swept them along the shore until they had almost reached the high-rise hotels. Quickly they jumped out. The usually green waves were now ugly brown, filled with dirt and sand that rubbed Alyssa's legs like sandpaper. Ty tried to drag the raft behind him, but the angry waves jerked it out of his hands. He let it go.

As they sloshed through the murky water that covered Stewart Beach, the waves slapped their backsides, making them stumble. Soon Alyssa felt tall grass under her feet instead of the smooth white beach sand. As they reached Seawall Boulevard, Alyssa saw something shiny on top of a big rock jutting above the waterline. It was a seashell—a perfect mouse cowrie—just like the kind that her grandfather had always looked for but never found. The storm must have carried it from the Caribbean. She quickly slid the brown spotted shell into the pocket of her shorts before the next wave could sweep it away. If she lived to tell her story, it would make a nice souvenir of Hurricane Berta.

They were still at least ten miles from Captain Mac's stables. There was no possible way to walk that distance before the full force of the hurricane would hit in a couple of hours. Their only hope was to find someone in a four-wheeler or truck going that way.

As far as the eyes could see, the road was covered with a layer of water. Trees dipped to the ground in gusts, then sprang up in the lulls. The boulevard was deserted. Here and there cars had been abandoned on the side of the road or in parking lots, but no people were out. Several blocks away, the waves crashed against the seawall like cannons, exploding into white foam as they slammed against the granite boulders at its base. Alyssa could hardly hear Ty's words as he cupped his hands over his mouth and yelled.

"We'd better give it up and find shelter. One of those hotels should be safe."

But Alyssa had seen something ahead. She shook her head and ran into the wind. Ty cursed, grabbed Dylan's hand, and followed her.

One block later, she found what she was looking for—a green telephone truck with flashing yellow lights. Two men in tan uniforms were removing a small tree that had blown against a telephone pole and gotten caught in the lines.

"You kids gets back!" one of the men shouted and waved them away. They waited until the tree was cleared and the men had returned to their truck.

"What are you doing out here?" the tall one asked as he removed his thick rubber gloves. "Where do you live?"

"Down off of Termini Road," Ty said. "We were trying to get home. Can you give us a lift?"

The men exchanged glances and shook their heads in mutual disbelief.

"Okay, get in," the short one said. He lifted Dylan over a deep mud puddle. They all scrunched into the front seat of the truck, Dylan in Alyssa's lap and Ty in the short man's lap.

The truck moved slowly down the boulevard, heading west. As the winds blew harder, the debris crashed against the truck's side. Mostly it was sand, small rocks, loose lumber, and trash. A limp newspaper blew across the windshield, stuck a few seconds, then ripped away.

Making good time, they finally reached the farm road. But suddenly the truck stopped. The road ahead was blocked by ropes with a Road Closed sign attached and two wooden barricades. About two inches of water covered the road and some of the lowest pastures, making the west end of the island look like a shallow lake. There was no way for the truck to get around the barricade without going into deep, muddy ditches.

"Sorry, kids, this is as far as we can go. How much farther is it to your house?"

Ty scratched his head and turned to Alyssa. She pointed to Uncle D's little café just down the road. Quickly she climbed down from the truck, pulling Dylan with her.

"Thanks for your help," Ty called out as he shook hands with the men. "We're almost home. Don't worry about us."

"Stay away from any downed power lines!" the tall man warned as he opened the door. Wind rushed in like a roaring train. "Get to a shelter now! This flying debris can kill you!"

The man didn't have to tell Alyssa twice. She vividly remembered the stories Uncle D had told her about people being cut in half from flying shards of glass during hurricanes. Although the worst of the storm hadn't arrived yet, it was foolish to be out in it. She knew that all too well. Mud oozed up over their shoes and ankles as they stepped onto the road. Carefully they picked their way between the boards, sticks, plastic, and miscellaneous items blown from people's porches or yards and now scattered in the road.

Dylan stumbled several times. Ty picked him up and carried him on his strong shoulders, which was not easy because the wind pushed them like a big, wet hand. Alyssa's long hair whipped into her eyes and mouth and wrapped around her neck. She tried to stuff it into her raincoat, but the effort was useless. The cool air made her teeth chatter and she couldn't stop the violent shaking.

Through the pouring rain, Uncle D's small café stood out like a lost puppy, looking sad and lonely. His favorite weeping willow tree swayed in a wild dance, and all his beautiful summer rosebushes had been stripped down to naked branches and thorns. White and pink petals from his oleander bushes stuck all over the soaked sheets of plywood nailed over his windows and door.

All along the road, young tallow trees covered with white waxy berries had snapped in two and their branches had blown against the café's front door. When the threesome reached the small building, they dodged into the carport that was attached to Uncle D's tiny brick house behind the café. As they gasped for air and shook uncontrollably, Alyssa noticed that Uncle D's Jeep Cherokee was not there. And for the first time, now that she was out of the pounding rain, she realized that her head was throbbing with pain.

"Let's try calling your grandfather," Ty shouted. "There's a phone booth at the corner of the café."

Alyssa shook her head. Some teenagers had vandalized that phone booth months ago and it was still out of order.

"What about your house, Curly?" Ty asked Dylan.

The boy shrugged and wiped the water from his face. His glasses were missing, probably at the bottom of the sea by now.

"It's too far away to walk. Can't we just stay here?"

"Maybe," Ty replied as he tapped on the side

of the building. "This place looks pretty sturdy. It must have been through a lot of storms in its day. If we could just figure out how to get inside." He pulled on the doorknob. The door didn't budge. He examined the plywood nailed securely over the windows.

Ty may have been right about Uncle D's house being safe, but all Alyssa could think about was her grandfather and the horses. Uncle D must have gone to the stables to pick up Captain Mac. Wherever they were, they would be together, she was sure of that. But if they had planned to ride out the storm in Uncle D's house, surely they would have returned by now. Maybe they were at Uncle Steven's house. Or maybe they were at the police station filing a missing person report.

Worst of all, maybe they had been so busy worrying about Dylan they had forgotten about getting the horses to higher ground. That last thought filled Alyssa with uneasiness. She had to find out if the horses were safe, and if not, do everything she could to save them.

She didn't have a dry notepad and she didn't have the time to use hand gestures to explain to Ty what she wanted to do. She didn't expect him to understand her or to stick with her. She pushed Dylan into Ty's hands and started walking back toward the main road.

"Where are you going, Blondie?" Ty shouted, just as she had expected he would. She jabbed her finger toward the west, where the stables lay.

"You are the stubbornest girl I've ever met," he yelled at her back. "It's safe here. Down that road we don't know what might happen. Those old stables are too dangerous. Come back!"

"Alyssa, don't leave me here!" Dylan shouted in a high-pitched squeal. "You promised to look after me."

Alyssa didn't stop. She couldn't take the time to try to communicate. The worst of the storm was yet to come. The rain was steady now and felt like tiny hailstones pelting her raincoat. The water wasn't sweet like regular rainwater but salty like the sea. It burned her eyes and stung her bare legs beneath the popping, crackling plastic slicker. The wind had increased and would continue to do so until the eye of the storm hit. Already Alyssa was finding it difficult to stand up. If she did not find the horses within the next hour, there would be little hope of saving them. After that the wind and rain would be too dangerous, and airborne debris would be as deadly as flying knives.

It was evening now, and the setting sun was blocked out by the low gray clouds, making it darker and more gloomy than before. As Alyssa crept along the road, holding onto anything she could for support, her brain whirred. She thought about how everything she did turned into pain or trouble for someone. Her grandfather was miserable because of the way she acted in school; her aunt and uncle were unhappy because she couldn't talk; Dylan and Ty were stuck in the middle of a hurricane because of her; and her parents had probably been lost because of something she had done. Why was she the one who kept on surviving, while others around her suffered?

If only she could do something constructive once in her life, maybe the streak of bad luck would end. Alyssa's fingers sought out and found the golden locket around her neck. It had helped her great-grandmother survive the Great Hurricane of 1900. Maybe it would bring her good luck, too.

At that moment Alyssa made up her mind that she would save the horses, no matter what the cost to herself. Maybe saving them would make up for all the trouble she had caused the people she loved the most. Ty and Dylan called after her, but she could not stop. This was the one thing she had to do.

Chapter Fourteen

THOSE

IN

PERIL

The cold rain and howling wind sent shivers through Alyssa's body. Her heart pounded against her ribs and pain throbbed in her head.

She grabbed anything at hand to help her make her way down the road—shrubs, wild canes, or an occasional fence. After going about fifty yards, she heard a shout behind her.

"Blondie! Wait for us!"

Alyssa saw Ty waving frantically from a ditch that now looked like a swamp. Dylan stood over the short boy tugging at his arm. Alyssa ran to Ty and pulled him out of the hole he had stepped into. Mud coated his body from the waist down, making him look like some kind of monster.

"Let's hold hands," Ty suggested as he caught his breath. Alyssa took one hand and Dylan took the other. All of their hands were slippery, making it difficult to hang on. The wind pushed their backs like an angry bully forcing them to trot to keep from being shoved to the ground. Although they were tired and out of breath, they had no choice but to keep moving.

Along the road, summerhouses creaked on their stilts and shingles flipped off. A few of the poorly built houses, or ones still under construction, had given in to the wind already. Plywood flapped where nails had not been hammered in well, and small trees planted in the spring rolled across the yards. Boats that hadn't been properly secured—mostly those of people who lived far away—had flipped over onto their sides in driveways or slid across the road into the marshes. The electric company had already cut off the power to prevent fires and electrocutions, sinking the island in eerie darkness. As far as Alyssa could tell, nearly everyone on the west end had evacuated for higher ground. The three longhorn cattle she had seen being loaded into trailers were gone.

The closer they came to the ocean, the deeper the water. At last they saw Captain Mac's stables. With a burst of energy, they dashed to the low wood building and ducked inside. It was empty.

"Where are all the horses?" Ty asked as he leaned against a stall door, catching his breath. Waist-deep water covered the sandy floor. Brushes and pieces of tack floated about, bumping against the stalls. A couple of dead fish had lodged in the hay. Outside, the waves beat continuously against the walls.

"Are we going to stay here?" Dylan asked, then collapsed on top of the metal feed bin. He pressed his back against a bale of hay. "I'm too tired to go any farther."

Ty sloshed through the water and sat beside Dylan.

"Hey, Curly, you're doing great. I've never seen a braver kid than you. It's gonna be all right." He squeezed Dylan's shoulders. The boy smiled sheepishly.

After a few moments of rest, the three ran to Captain Mac's shack. The screen door hung by one hinge and rattled wildly. The kitchen window-pane lay in shattered pieces in the sink. True to his word, Captain Mac had not boarded the place up this time. The back door was not even locked, so Alyssa jerked it open and stepped into the dark, empty kitchen. The curtains over the sink looked like wet rags flapping in the wind.

"Where is your granddaddy?" Ty asked. "Where are the horses? Do you think that man from Freeport already picked them up?"

Alyssa hurried to her bedroom and removed a dry sheet of paper and a ballpoint pen from her dresser. Quickly she scribbled: "High ground. I have to go there." She underlined the word "have" so Ty would understand that she had no intention of staying in the shack. Besides, the way the shingles were flying off, and the walls were shaking and swaying with each sudden gust of wind, she didn't think the shack would last through the storm. The waves were getting higher. Their constant pounding might wash the piers out from under the house.

After reading the note, Ty eased his body down onto the worn sofa where Dylan was already sitting.

"Oh, no," Ty groaned, and passed the note to Dylan. "Maybe Hal was right after all, Blondie. Maybe you *are* crazy."

Any other time, Alyssa might have kicked Ty's shins, but she didn't have time to waste. She stood, hands on her hips, glaring at Ty, who was stretched out on the couch, working his legs behind Dylan's back.

"Can't we just stay here for a while? I'm too tired to move." Ty closed his eyes and propped his head on the armrest.

"Yeah, we're too tired to move," Dylan mimicked as he laid his head on the opposite armrest.

"Besides," Ty said, opening one eye, "your grandpappy *must* be all right. And the horses, too. I'm too tired to go back into that storm. Let's ride it out here."

Alyssa shook her head stubbornly and pointed to the barometer on the wall. The pressure registered 29.5 inches and was falling. She knew they had very little time before it would be impossible to go back outside. The wind would hurl debris at them and rip at their clothes. Even though the thermometer registered 82 degrees, the cool rain and fierce wind made the temperature feel much lower.

"Leave us alone," Ty muttered as Alyssa tried to pull him up.

Uncertainty crept over Alyssa as she stared at the two boys. More than ever she wished she could speak. She needed to tell them that the shack was unsafe. If the hurricane hit the west side of the island, the waves and wind would smash the little house and stables to pieces, or the storm surge would wash them away. Captain Mac had evacuated the house and stables many times over the years and always seemed surprised to see them still standing afterward. This could be the day that the luck of the little house ran out.

Alyssa's lips moved. The sound of a word traveled up her throat toward her mouth. It was an emergency; surely that iron vise clamping her throat would let go just this one time. But no, the words froze in her larynx, turning into a squeak. She clenched her fists and slammed them on the kitchen tabletop.

"Whoa!" Ty said, sitting up. "Take it easy, girl. What's wrong now?"

Alyssa had a strong hunch that her grandfather and Uncle D were holing up in the old shelter in an abandoned cow pasture. It was a sturdy building that had endured forty years of storms. The original owner had brought in truckloads of dirt to raise the ground level. He built his sturdy barn on top of the hill so his valuable livestock would be safe from high water. About forty yards away, on another little hill, sat his shelter, which contained emergency supplies and a stockpile of food. Very few people stayed on the west end during hurricanes, but if they ever did get trapped, the shelter was available to anyone who needed it. Alyssa knew that if Captain Mac and Uncle D were still on the island, they would probably be there. And if the horses had not been taken away by the man from Freeport, more than likely they would be in the nearby barn.

Alyssa grabbed the sheet of paper again and wrote: "Not safe here. Shelter on higher ground. Let's go." She shoved the note under Ty's nose. He moaned but slowly rose to his feet. Dylan did the same.

"Okay, okay," Ty mumbled. "But I swear that is the last place I'm dragging this body of mine. I'll just let the wind carry me to the Land of Oz."

Alyssa grabbed two flashlights from the hall closet. One was the heavy-duty kind like firemen or policemen use. It had belonged to her father. Its powerful beam lit up the living room when she flipped on the switch. She handed it to Ty and Dylan, keeping the smaller one for herself.

As the three of them stepped out the back door, the first thing they saw was the dark wall of water that once had been the beautiful green sea. Though it was dark outside, Alyssa sensed that the waves were as high as the stable roof. They smashed against the sand dunes, bringing tree limbs, seaweed, fish and jellyfish, and trash from miles away. The roar and hiss was frightening, yet in a way the drama was beautiful and exciting to Alyssa. Her heart pounded with the surf as she stood mesmerized. She wanted to stay, but there was no time. Already the water had risen to the middle of the concrete steps leading to the house's back door.

They crossed Termini Road and headed north down a small side road that led inland to the shelter. They held onto anything they could find, mostly shrubs and small trees. In places the water was waist high, and once it was so deep they had to swim. They kept their eyes open for snakes every inch of the way. In a great storm, snakes might be anywhere, even in trees. Alyssa felt a sharp pain in her right leg. When she shone the light on it, she saw that she had scraped against a piece of barbed-wire fence.

Alyssa didn't want Dylan to see what they came across next. It was gruesome, so she tried to stand between him and the animal carcass. They had already passed some dead birds, a rabbit, a chicken, and an armadillo. Now she saw a cow caught in the barbed-wire fence and stuck in deep mud. Only the animal's head peered above the water, swaying lifelessly.

At last they saw the dark form of the solid brick building on top of the man-made knoll. Alyssa directed the flashlight beam on the barn and saw the outline of several horses huddled under an open-ended barn made from sturdy poles. She recognized Stormy's gray body and his familiar whinny. Alyssa smiled and sighed with relief. Ty cheered.

"Looks like you were right," he said. "The horses are okay."

Alyssa nodded. As long as they remained in the barn on the high ground, they would be all right.

Ty pounded on the heavy metal door of the brick building for a long time before it opened. Uncle D peered out, squinting through the blasting sheets of rain.

"Lordy Almighty! What happened to you? Your grandfather has gone crazy with worry." He stepped aside as the children came in out of the storm.

As Uncle D closed the door, silence rang in Alyssa's ears. For a minute she couldn't hear anything he said because of the blood pounding in her eardrums. Then slowly the sound of the wailing wind and rattling roof returned. The only light in the dark, musty building came from some candles and a Coleman lantern. An elderly couple sat on a cot pushed against the far wall next to stacks of boxes and canned food. Anxiously, they listened to the news on a portable radio. A woman with two toddlers huddled on another cot piled high with blankets and dry clothes. But Captain Mac was not there. Alyssa spun around and searched Uncle D's eyes.

"Your grandfather isn't here, Alyssa. The derned old fool went out looking for you and Dylan. He was sure you'd come back to the stables. I tried to stop him, but he was too ornery. He stole my Jeep and headed down the road. With that crippled leg of his, he won't be able to control the car. I tried to call the police, but the phone lines are down all over."

"What about our aunt and uncle?" Dylan asked in a shaky voice. "Did they go with Captain Mac?"

"Nope. I don't know exactly where they are right now. And let me tell you, they're sick with worry, sonny. They already went to the police."

Alyssa started for the door, but Uncle D grabbed her arm.

"Why don't you children get out of those wet clothes. There are some dry things over on the cot. I've got some hot soup and coffee fixed up." He put his gnarled hand on Alyssa's back, but she broke free and returned to the door.

"Hey, Blondie, where are you going now? We're finally safe, aren't we?" Ty asked, then slurped from a cup of soup the old woman had handed him.

Alyssa couldn't find a sheet of paper, so she

borrowed Uncle D's pen and wrote on the side of one of the cardboard boxes: "Must find Grandpa. You can stay. Thanks for help."

Ty glanced at the box, shook his head, and hissed air between his teeth.

"You *are* the stubbornest girl I've ever met, I'll say that much for you. But you know I can't let you go out in this storm again. It's worse than before."

Alyssa knew Ty was right, but it didn't matter. She eased the door open and felt the cold blast of water and wind punch her face. She waded to the pole barn. Stormy neighed softly and pushed his wet gray nose against her stomach. He still wore his halter and a long lead rope, just as when she had left him.

Alyssa climbed onto Stormy's damp back. It felt warm against her bare, trembling legs. As she steered Stormy back to the narrow road, she saw Ty running out of the shelter, his head tucked to his chest as if he were dodging bullets. He ran to Stormy and held one hand up to Alyssa. She took the flashlight from his hand, then helped him climb up behind her.

"I can't believe I'm on top of old Trigger again," he muttered as he wrapped his arms around Alyssa's waist.

She guided Stormy out onto the road. As his

hooves sank into the layer of mud and silt on top of the pavement, he whinnied in protest. She urged him on, patting his neck. Never before had she asked so much of the little mustang, and she wouldn't have been surprised to see him balk and refuse to go into the storm. But Stormy wasn't just her horse, he was her friend. He seemed to sense that something was terribly wrong and that he was needed. Without further complaint, he began to trot.

They headed back toward Captain Mac's house, this time taking a different route—a wider, paved road that the Jeep would have taken. When they reached the turnoff onto Termini Road, they saw a dark rectangular form that looked like a car. Ty raised the powerful flashlight and pointed its beam toward the motionless vehicle.

Alyssa struggled to scream. Ty groaned.

"Oh no!" he said, but the wind ripped the words from his mouth.

The Jeep lay on its side, with the driver's door slung open. On the ground beside the car Captain Mac lay as still as death.

Chapter Fifteen

BERTA

ARRIVES

Alyssa felt sick inside. Her knees trembled and she doubted that she could walk the few feet to the overturned car. But Ty did not hesitate. He leapt off Stormy and ran to the old man's motionless body. Ty gently rolled Captain Mac over. He placed an ear to the pale, dirt-splattered lips and pressed his hand over the old man's heart.

"He's still alive!" Ty shouted, and waved Alyssa over.

Alyssa didn't want to go closer; she didn't want

to see her grandfather's face. But she forced her legs to move. Mud coated his white beard and plastered it to his face, but the driving rain soon washed the mud away. The navy blue cap was off, revealing the bald circle on his crown. Suddenly Alyssa felt embarrassed for the old man, having his secret exposed to the world. She resolved to replace the cap as soon as they got him to safety.

"We have to get him back to the shelter," Ty said. "Can we lift him up onto your horse?"

Alyssa shook her head. She and Ty were small. And even though Ty's muscles rippled as he lifted the body, Captain Mac was too tall and heavy for them. After a few minutes of struggling, Ty cursed and lay the man back down.

"It's no use. We can't lift him that high. Our only chance to save him is to get the car back upright and drive him to the shelter."

They walked around the Jeep Cherokee into a ditch of waist-high water and pushed the car with all their combined strength. With a squeak and a crunch, the car rolled upright and rocked gently. They quickly lifted Captain Mac onto the backseat. But when Ty settled into the driver's seat and started the engine, the back tires spun in the air and sent water flying.

Ty got out and examined the rear tires. They hung suspended over the deep ditch filled with water. The front tires were sunk in water and deep mud. Ty muttered and kicked the back bumper.

"Let's try to push one of the back tires onto solid ground." The rain fell into Ty's mouth as he spoke, making his words sound garbled, as if he were talking in a shower.

He showed Alyssa how to brace her back against the car. On his signal they grunted and pushed with all their might. The car moved forward about two inches, then slid back toward the ditch. Ty cursed. They tried again two more times, but the deep water won the battle.

"All right, you get into the driver's seat and step on the gas pedal while I push," Ty said as he wiped the rain from his eyes.

Alyssa did as told, but still the tires would not move. As Alyssa helped Ty put pieces of lumber and debris under the front tires in hopes of creating some traction, she felt a shove at her back. She turned to see Stormy shaking his head. He often did this when he was feeling playful, but this time he seemed to be telling her something. Without thinking, Alyssa unfastened Stormy's long lead rope and retied it around his neck, then handed the loose end to Ty.

Ty shrugged. "Well, it's worth a try." He tied the rope to the Cherokee's front bumper, then got behind the steering wheel.

"Go," he yelled. Alyssa clucked to Stormy and tugged on the halter. The rope stretched tight. Stormy stopped. Ty shouted, and Alyssa urged the horse forward again. The rope dug into Stormy's chest, but he kept on walking as the car slowly rolled forward. With a gurgle, the front tires came out of the deep mud and the car slid sideways across the road, almost going into the opposite ditch. Alyssa threw her arms around Stormy's neck and pressed her face to his warm skin.

"You did it, Blondie!" Ty cheered.

When Alyssa removed the rope from Stormy's neck, she saw a raw, red groove cut into his gray hide. She stroked him gently and kissed his nose, then swung up on his back and pointed toward the road they had just come down.

"Okay, let's move it." Ty gave the thumbs-up signal, then awkwardly steered the boxy-looking car onto the road. He could have used a phone book to sit on, for his eyes barely reached above the dashboard. Alyssa rode behind, watching the taillights weave from side to side. Sometimes it looked as if the car would slide into the ditch again, but somehow Ty managed to reach the shelter.

The wind was merciless now. It caught one of the car doors and slung it open, exposing Captain Mac to a shower of cold rain. Uncle D trotted out carrying an umbrella, his face pale and his eyes wide with fright. The wind whipped the umbrella inside out and tore at Uncle D's clothes as he held onto the door.

"Lordy, what happened to Mac?"

"The car turned over. Looks like he hit his head on something. It's bleeding," Ty explained. While Ty and Uncle D carried the unconscious man inside and placed him on an empty cot, Alyssa quickly returned Stormy to the barn. Uncle D was outside for only a few minutes, but the driving rain had soaked his clothes as if he'd dived into the ocean. Ty moved the Jeep to the leeward side of the shelter for protection.

"We've got to get him to the hospital," Uncle D said as Ty entered the room.

"Isn't that too risky?" Ty asked. "The hurricane is going full force right now. I don't think we could make it all the way to the hospital, do you?"

"I guess you're right, son. I've got a first-aid kit over here. At least we can get that wound cleaned up."

While Uncle D searched for his kit, Alyssa found two navy blankets and laid them over her grandfather. Then she rolled up a towel and placed it under his head for a pillow. The blood trickled in a thin red line down his temple. Gently she placed the blue cap over his bald spot and tenderly stroked his white beard.

Uncle D dabbed the wound with antiseptic, then wrapped a gauze bandage around Captain Mac's head. Immediately a small spot of red soaked through the white cloth.

"It's a deep cut," Uncle D said sadly. "I told the old fool not to go out in the storm. With his bum leg I knew he wouldn't be able to control the brakes. But he took off while my back was turned. He was so worried about you and your little brother. The derned old fool." His voice cracked.

Uncle D's fingers trembled as he wiped some of the water and mud from Captain Mac's face and neck. Alyssa recalled the tall tales the two old men had shared. Uncle D had saved her grandfather's life in World War II. She wondered if he would be able to do it again.

Captain Mac's hand felt cold to the touch and his lips were bluish. Alyssa scooted her metal folding chair closer to his cot and watched his chest rise and fall. Ty made her remove her wet slicker, then wrapped a blanket around her shoulders, but still she shook. Later, Uncle D patted her head softly.

"Why don't you join Dylan and the others and

eat something? There's nothing we can do until the storm lets up," he said. Alyssa hardly heard his voice over the howling wind that sounded almost human as it rattled the windowless building.

She shook her head and pulled Captain Mac's hand closer to her chest. Across the room the old couple had set up a Coleman stove. They had warmed up a can of pork and beans and some to-mato soup over a small Sterno stove and had poured warm soda pop into plastic cups for the toddlers.

Alyssa was glad to see that Dylan looked com-fortable and relaxed now. He slurped soup while he listened to Ty tell how they had rescued Captain Mac. Ty waved his hands, casting tall shadows on the wall. Changing his expression from time to time and whinnying like a horse, he made Dylan and the small children laugh freely. Alyssa didn't mind him getting all the attention. He had helped to save her grandfather's life and as soon as every-thing had settled down, she was going to thank him somehow. Maybe a new tackle box or a fancy fishing lure.

Alyssa wished that she shared the faith of the others in the room that everything would be all right. But she could feel her grandfather's hands turning colder and his pulse getting weaker as time passed.

After everyone had eaten, the old woman came

up with the idea of singing church hymns. Ty didn't know many of the words, but that didn't stop him from trying. The old woman's voice was high and quivery, and she wouldn't let go of a note even after everyone else was ready to move on. The woman's husband and Uncle D had nice, warm voices. It brought back memories to Alyssa of all the times she had sat on the back pew at the Island Church during the hot summer nights. The windows were usually kept open because the old church didn't have air-conditioning. If a cool breeze came off the ocean, it wasn't so bad, except for June bugs crashing in, usually to the relief of some bored child.

Alyssa sang along in her mind. She wondered if her voice had changed in the past three years. Her mother had been a lovely alto. The last time Alyssa had sung, her own voice had been high and childish. Would it still be that way now or would it be more mature? she wondered. Alyssa moved her lips and tried to form the words to the songs, but nothing came out. Maybe the doctors had been wrong. After all, she had remembered parts of what had happened that day when the charter boat went down. She had remembered sneaking aboard and being in the life raft. She had partial memories of that day, so why then didn't she have at least a partial voice?

When the old couple started singing the hymn that Alyssa's mother had loved the most, she felt a lump rise to her throat and had to turn away from the others. She tried to concentrate on the wind and the rain hammering the walls and the sound of shingles popping off one by one. But still, she heard the song.

Alyssa tried to think about the horses. They would get wet, of course. If by some chance one of them broke away, it might try to jump the fence or stumble in the mud. But the barn was sturdy and high. It had been protecting horses and cows for many more years than Alyssa had lived. She knew that as long as the animals stayed in the barn, they would be safe.

But it was hard for her to think about the horses and the storm when she looked at Captain Mac's pale face. Now his lips moved as if he were trying to speak, but when Alyssa leaned closer, her long hair touching his chest, she could not hear his breathless words. Gently she combed his white beard with a piece of broken comb she had found on the floor.

After the singing stopped, Dylan curled up on one of the cots. He had changed into some dry clothes—a pair of ratty jeans and a man's shirt that hung past his knees. Ty had found a dry

T-shirt with a picture of a surfboard and palm trees on the front of it. Wrapped in a pink flannel blanket, he walked over to Alyssa and squatted beside her chair.

"You haven't eaten anything today, have you? You must be starving. Want me to fix you a bowl of soup?"

Alyssa knew he was right. She felt too weak to move, and her body ached from bailing water and paddling the lifeboat and from fighting the strong wind and water. She was exhausted, and even breathing caused some pain. But she shook her head.

"Going hungry won't help your grandpappy, you know."

Alyssa shot him an angry glance. How could Ty understand how she felt? No one could, because no one knew that she was the cause of so much pain. Wasn't it her fault that her grandfather was hurt, just as it had been her fault that her mother had died and her father had been lost at sea?

Tears collected in the corners of Alyssa's eyes, and her nose started to run. She tried not to sniff but finally had to. Ty put his arms around her shivering shoulders and hugged her. His small body felt warm.

"Don't worry, your grandpappy will be okay. We'll get him to the hospital as soon as the storm slacks off."

Ty's hand resting on Alyssa's shoulder felt like a pound of lead to her. She wanted to shrug it off, not because she was mad at him but because she didn't feel deserving of his comfort. She didn't deserve his or Uncle D's or the old couple's kindness. Why couldn't they see that Captain Mac was dying because of her?

Alyssa stood and walked to the boxes of provisions. She fiddled around until she found a can of dried almonds. Behind the stack of boxes she changed into some pink-colored jeans and a yellow shirt with a teddy bear on the pocket. Avoiding sitting under a crack in the ceiling where rainwater dripped in, she slumped against the damp wall. The concrete felt icy cold on her legs. The wall rumbled and vibrated behind her, making her feel as if she were riding an old locomotive. As music from an oldies station on the portable radio gently filled the air, Alyssa leaned back and closed her eyes.

It was Ty who first noticed the change in Captain Mac. Ty suddenly rose to his feet, leaned over the cot, and placed his hand on the old man's forehead.

"He's burning up with fever. His face is covered with sweat."

Alyssa shook off her stupor, mad at herself for not noticing that the beads of water on Captain Mac's face were not raindrops as she'd thought.

"You're right, son. He's getting worse," Uncle D said as he placed his hand on the sweaty brow.

"Maybe we should try the car," Ty suggested. "The storm seems to be letting up, don't you think? Listen to the wind."

Ty cracked the heavy door open.

"Hey, I think I see the moon. Come look, Alyssa."

Alyssa stepped to his side. He was right. The rain had slowed, and the moon and two dim stars peeped between some wispy clouds. She pushed the door open all the way, letting in a blast of cool, crisp air.

"Hold on a minute," Uncle D called out as he shuffled after them. "That's just the eye of the harrycane passing over. It'll be hitting us again in a little while from the other direction, harder than ever. If you get stuck in the storm, you might get swept away. All of you might get killed."

"But we've got to try," Ty said. "Captain Mac may die if he doesn't get to a hospital. Let's at least try to get him down the road to a telephone and call an ambulance."

Uncle D resisted, but after glancing at Captain Mac's flushed face one more time, he agreed. All three of them carried the unconscious man to the car and put him on the backseat. Alyssa wanted Dylan to stay in the shelter, but he cried and started coughing, so she finally gave in and let him come, too.

Ty and Uncle D argued over who would drive, but finally they decided that Uncle D's experience was more important than Ty's strength for the journey ahead. Uncle D slid into the driver's seat while Ty climbed onto the hood.

"I'll be your navigator," he shouted as the car began to slowly roll toward the road.

Alyssa crossed her fingers. Early that morning the weatherman had said that the eye of Hurricane Berta was about twenty miles wide. It might take almost an hour to pass by, or it might take only twenty minutes, depending on the speed of the hurricane. They might have enough time to get to a hospital, or they might all get caught in the middle of Berta's fury. The worst might be over, or the worst might be yet to come.

Chapter Sixteen

THE

EYE OF

THE STORM

The car moved so slowly, Alyssa could hardly stand it. But at least they were moving, doing something, and no longer just waiting. Wedged between Uncle D and Dylan, Alyssa turned on the radio. The deejay was warning people not to go outside because the storm wasn't over and because tornadoes were touching down in the area. That news was even more frightening to her than hurricanes, for tornado winds were stronger and hit without warning or reason.

"Better take Termini Road," Ty called out. "It's higher than Stewart Road."

Uncle D nodded and shouted, "Okay." As they drove, Alyssa felt as if they were in a black bottomless pit. The only light came from the Jeep headlights, the full moon, and an occasional lantern in someone's house. Water flowed like rivers in the ditches that could not be distinguished from the road itself. Ty shone the flashlight and carefully marked where the road signs and fence posts were. He constantly shouted, "to the left a little" or "to the right" or "take it slow here." Debris and dead animals and some live snakes floated on top of the water, making the going even more difficult. But somehow the sturdy Jeep managed to get past all obstacles.

"Old Red can make it," Uncle D would say as he squinted at the bright headlights reflecting on the water. "Slowly now, just a few more feet. Come on, old girl, you can do it." Then he would grin and pat the dashboard as if the car were his faithful dog.

Flocks of birds flew overhead, caught in the eye and unable to get out. A few stopped to rest briefly on telephone lines, waiting for the edge of the vortex wall to arrive. One of them was a brightly colored parrot. It must have flown all the way from the Caribbean within Berta's calm eye.

At last they reached the security of Seawall Boulevard. Only a few cars were out on the wide street—mostly city vehicles, ambulances, and four-wheelers driven by good Samaritans looking for accidents and stranded people to help.

Once on this main artery, Uncle D pressed the accelerator. The red car surged forward, its powerful motor humming and its exhaust pipe billowing. The seventeen-foot seawall protected this road from the ocean and made the going faster. The car bumped over stray scraps of lumber and plywood, but most of the debris had blown across the boulevard and lodged against the walls of the shops, hotels, and restaurants. All the while they moved, Alyssa glanced out the window at the sky, praying that they would reach the hospital before the fury of the hurricane's vortex passed over them again. Ten minutes later they arrived at Twelfth Street, one of the turnoffs that led to the vast medical district at the east end of the city.

Alyssa wasn't sure how long the trek had taken, but the sky to the south had turned dark again, and some wispy clouds now covered the moon. The rain and wind started up again as they pulled into the emergency entrance of the first hospital they came to. While Uncle D honked the horn and eased the car close to the doors, Ty jumped out and dashed inside the building. Soon two orderlies dressed in white charged out the door, pushing a gurney. They hoisted Captain Mac onto the stretcher and vanished through the wide doors.

Alyssa sighed with relief, and a sudden overwhelming sensation of exhaustion swept over her. Her knees buckled, and the last thing she remembered was falling on the cold, slick sidewalk.

Alyssa awakened in the waiting room, stretched out on an imitation-leather sofa. Ty sat next to her, drinking a cold Coke and munching a bag of potato chips. Uncle D sipped steaming coffee from a Styrofoam cup. Alyssa moved her leg, only to feel it stick to the plastic seat. As she pried it loose and sat up, Dylan moaned in his sleep in the chair next to her.

Ty offered the bag of chips.

"How do you feel?"

Alyssa shrugged and looked around the waiting room packed with tourists in swimsuits or flowered shirts. Most appeared to be suffering from minor cuts and sprains. Others had come to wait out news of more serious accidents. Ty told her that a child had fallen into a swollen drainage ditch; a teenager had a punctured lung from a piece of flying window glass; and two older people had suffered heart attacks in the excitement of evacuation. Even as he spoke, she heard the wail of a siren approaching the hospital.

Alyssa watched the hands creep forward on the overhead clock. Outside the wind howled like Godzilla. Bricks and tree limbs and loose debris thumped against the building walls and scraped over the roof. And between all these sounds came the roar of the waves crashing against the seawall a few blocks away.

Alyssa tried to concentrate on some *National Geographic* magazines she'd picked up from the lamp stand. She examined the seascapes hanging on the wall, but each time a nurse or doctor entered the waiting room, she jumped.

At last a plump doctor with a bald head fringed by curly hair opened the door and approached Uncle D. Alyssa's heart skipped a beat, then raced as she looked into the man's tired, drawn face.

"Is he gone?" Uncle D asked calmly, rising to his feet.

"No. He's still hanging on. But it doesn't look good."

"What are his chances, doctor?"

"Frankly speaking, I'd say about fifty-fifty right now. He's not stabilizing as much as we'd like. He's delirious and keeps mumbling about someone being dead because of him. Someone named Alyssa."

Alyssa scooted to the edge of the sofa.

"Why, this is Alyssa right here, doctor. She's not dead. This is his granddaughter. She's the one who found him and helped bring him here. Poor old Mac. I guess he figured she was lost in the harrycane. You see, he lost his only son in a storm three years ago and hasn't really been the same since."

The doctor's eyebrows crinkled as he turned to Alyssa.

"You may be the only one who can help him through this crisis, Alyssa." He gently took her arm as she rose to her feet. "We've done all we can do medically. Living is now a matter of will, and that's the one thing he doesn't have. He needs you to tell him that you're alive and well. That might give him the extra strength to boost him out of danger."

"Can I come, too?" Uncle D asked.

"Well, we shouldn't have so many people in there at one time—"

"But there's a big problem you don't know about." Uncle D lowered his voice to a whisper. "Alyssa can't speak. She's a mute. She can't tell Mac that she's alive."

The doctor's face flushed, then he drew in a deep breath.

"I see. All right, both of you come along."

Once inside her grandfather's room, Alyssa's heart pounded faster, the beat throbbing in her ears. The smell of medicine, the beep of the heart monitor, and the eerie tubes running around Captain Mac's arms and into his nose made her stomach feel heavy.

Captain Mac's face was almost as white as the clean bandages wrapped around his head. As his lips moved, his beard trembled softly, but his words were not understandable.

"Mac," Uncle D said as he leaned closer. "You old scalawag, dern you. I told you not to go out into the harrycane. Alyssa is all right, Mac. She's standing right here."

"Alyssa!" Captain Mac suddenly called out loudly. "The lass is gone. It's all my fault. She's gone—gone to the sea like my Robbie."

Tears crept from under his closed eyelids and trickled down his face. Then he was mumbling again.

"Alyssa, hold his hand," the doctor instructed.

As Alyssa took the cold hand into her own, her heart felt as if it would split her chest open, it thundered so. A sharp lump rose in her throat and she could not swallow it down. She opened her mouth, but as usual nothing came out.

"Go ahead and talk to him, child," Uncle D pleaded. "You can speak, I know you can. The doctors say there's nothing wrong with your voice box. Go ahead. For heaven's sake, you have to speak to him!"

Alyssa wanted to speak more than she ever had in the past three years. But the lock was frozen tight. Her throat throbbed as if a sledgehammer were pounding her larynx. She put her hands over her throat and with all her strength tried to force the words out. But nothing came.

Fear swelled up inside like an ocean wave and rolled over her. Terror smothered her. If she spoke, she knew something terrible would happen. But would it be any worse than having her grandfather die? If only she could remember and face that fear head on. Why, why couldn't she remember?

Everyone stared at Alyssa with such intent expressions, she felt like a sideshow freak. Suddenly Uncle D grabbed her shoulders and shook her hard.

"Try, child! Try harder!" His old voice cracked with emotion.

Alyssa could not bear it another moment. She twisted free and ran out into the corridor. Nurses and visitors and patients stared as she fled through the waiting room and out of the front doors streaked with duct tape to prevent the glass from shattering. Alyssa stopped under the breezeway that led to the parking garage, shivering from the cool rain and wind. In a trance, she stared at the hospital grounds and surrounding streets, which had become small lakes. Leaves and small tree limbs and sand and shingles swirled through the air. Palm trees whipped about, barely visible through the sheets of pounding rain. Some had already been uprooted and scooted across the yard like rolling pins. At the street intersection, the stop sign shook violently.

Very clearly Alyssa heard the ocean waves breaking against the shore a few blocks away. They boomed like cannons. Over the top of a nearby building she saw white spray shoot straight up into the dark sky. Rain swept under the rattling metal overhang and drenched Alyssa's face. It tasted like salty seawater and reminded her of the ocean. The waves out there would be high, sometimes thirty or forty feet. How could any human without a boat survive their pummeling?

Without warning, a scene flashed through Alyssa's mind, then another. She felt the memory monster awaken and begin to crawl out of its dark dungeon. It roared and scratched at the door, howling in unison with the raging wind. Alyssa squeezed her eyes shut and put her fingers in her ears to block out the whine and moan. But she knew it would do no good this time. The monster was going to get out, and it would either destroy her or set her free. Alyssa braced herself for battle.

She closed her eyes and took deep, slow breaths, allowing the memories to sweep over her. Soon the flashbacks came faster and faster. She was in her father's charter boat. Her mother had gone across the room to get some ropes. Her father was topside, furious because she had sneaked aboard. She was sick and wanted to throw up but had nothing left in her stomach. She heard her father shouting into the CB radio mouthpiece.

"I'm turning back," he had said. "I can't reach their yacht." That was just before the motor died. Her father tried again and again to start it, but the engine only chugged and shimmied and died. He called "mayday" over and over and gave out his coordinates. Someone replied, but the message was scratchy and weak. Then Alyssa heard something coming closer, like an eighteen-wheeler or a rumbling locomotive. She drew back the porthole curtain and saw a wall of green water. Then she felt the charter boat rise and roll. Her feet were suddenly not under her but over her head. Water gushed in through the open door.

"Alyssa!" her mother had shouted as the water slammed her back against the far wall. "Get upstairs! Hurry!" the woman cried.

Alyssa clung to the rail near the steps and tried to pull herself up, but the planks beneath her were too slippery. Foamy water rushed over her body. Then she saw her father's face above her in the doorway.

"Don't let go! Hold on while I unhook the dinghy," he yelled.

The boat tilted as the stern began to sink. Alyssa lost her grip and slid away. She grabbed the top bunk, which was still above the water level. Her mother was at the far end of the cabin. She hadn't moved since the water had swooped her against the wall. Only her shoulders and head protruded above the gurgling green water.

"Mommy, what's wrong?" Alyssa called out.

"Go with your father," the woman replied in a strained, weak voice.

A moment later Alyssa's father returned and swam through the water toward his daughter. He opened the top porthole, which was above the seawater, and pushed her through. Alyssa saw the dinghy tied only a few feet away, bumping against the side of the boat.

"Wait here while I get your mother," her father said, then disappeared below. Alyssa held on with both hands as the wind and water ravaged her face. It seemed forever before her father returned, his face white and his hair plastered to his head.

He gasped for air as he came up, and she knew he had been underwater.

"Get into the lifeboat," he said in a shaky voice, then helped Alyssa climb in. "Go to shore. I'll come along later. Your mother is caught on some ropes. I have to cut her loose."

Alyssa began crying and screaming. "Mommy! Mommy! We can't leave Mommy behind!"

"*Shh!*" Alyssa's father shook her. "I'm not leaving her. I'm going back below. Be quiet, Alyssa. Don't cry. You have to be brave. Hold onto the lifeboat as hard as you can. The Coast Guard will be here shortly."

"No, Daddy, don't make me go alone!" She wrapped her arms around his slippery neck and clung like a crab.

"*Shh!* Alyssa! Be quiet! Be brave and don't say another word. I promise you, it will be all right. I promise I'll join you later, but you have to be brave and don't cry or say a word."

Alyssa nodded and fought back the tears. He hugged her and kissed her, then untied the towrope from the boat.

"I love you, sweetheart!" he called out as he pushed the dinghy off into the churning water.

Alyssa started to cry and whimper. He put his finger to his lips.

"Remember your promise, Alyssa," he shouted over the whistling wind as the dinghy rocked away.

"I'll remember, Daddy," she called back as she watched him sink back under the water inside the boat. "I promise I won't say another word until you come home."

Alyssa's mind swirled with thoughts of her father as she stared across the flooded grounds of the hospital. She thought of everything she knew about him—from her first memory to her last. She saw him as a small boy riding along the beach in the arms of Lana Turner. She saw him grinning over the baseball trophy when his high school team won the state championship. She saw him laughing the day he gave her the green skiff and the day her mother christened the charter boat. And lastly, she remembered that day three years ago when his boat sank to the bottom of the sea. She saw her father's face, pale and wet as he shoved the dinghy off and told her to keep her promise, and the look in his eyes as he took a deep breath and vanished into the deep green water inside the boat.

Tears erupted from Alyssa's eyes and a choking sob racked her body. The truth ripped into her heart with a cruel slash and now it throbbed with pain. Her father was gone. Dead. He had died trying to save her mother and would never come back.

She had promised not to speak and he had promised to join her later. For three years she had kept the promise of a small, frightened child, believing he would return if she did not speak.

Alyssa did not fight the tears. She let them stream down her cheeks for several minutes with a rage that she had never felt before. She watched the rain strike the roofs across the street and listened to the thundering waves smashing against the shore. For a moment *she* was the storm.

Her sobs began to subside. Alyssa swallowed hard and rubbed her eyes. At last she knew exactly what she would do.

Chapter Seventeen

OUR

FATHER'S

MERCY

Inside the hospital, Alyssa took long, determined steps toward her grandfather's room. All faces turned to her as she burst through the door, but she didn't care who stared at her. She rushed to Captain Mac's bedside and took his pale hand into both of hers.

Pulling in a deep breath, she willed the words to come.

"Grandpa, I ..." A sudden sharp pain cut

into her throat, and she didn't recognize her own voice. It was too old and too hoarse and whispery.

"I'm sorry, Grandpa," she repeated as she pressed her face to his hand.

"She's talking!" Uncle D cried out in a raspy voice. "Bless the Lord, she's talking!"

"Alyssa, tell your grandfather that you're alive and well," the doctor whispered into her ear.

"Grandpa, it's Alyssa ... your granddaughter." She had to clear her throat over and over and swallow down the pain and the hoarseness. The doctor told the nurse to go get some throat spray, then he handed Alyssa a glass of water. She drank it, then turned back to Captain Mac.

"Grandpa? Can you hear me? It's not your fault I got caught in the hurricane. I wasn't really running away. I was mad because you were going to move and sell the horses. I didn't want you to go away, Grandpa, but it doesn't matter now. Now I just want you to get well."

Alyssa squeezed his hand and felt a weak response. She didn't know if he could hear her or if he recognized her hoarse, weak voice, but at least he wasn't mumbling any longer. The nurse returned and sprayed her throat with a medication, and soon Alyssa's voice grew stronger and the pain lessened.

"I promise not to make any more trouble. I won't get into fights at school. I'll do my homework and study real hard. I'll even wear dresses if you want me to. And look, Grandpa, I'm wearing the locket you gave me for my birthday. It's beautiful and it brought me good luck." She held the shiny locket to his face, but his eyes didn't open.

"Grandpa, you'll never guess what I found on the beach today—a mouse cowrie! You have to open your eyes to see it. Please open your eyes, Grandpa."

Alyssa lay her head on his chest. His heart beat too fast, and his breath was ragged. Then she felt a gentle touch on her head.

"Alyssa?" Captain Mac asked softly. "Are ye really talkin', lass?"

Alyssa raised her head, looked into his watery blue eyes, and smiled.

"Yes, I'm really talking, Grandpa. I'm doing it just for you." She squeezed his hand, and this time his grip felt firm.

"The Good Shepherd has brought you back to his flock, lassie," he said in a weak, shaky voice. "I'll be down on my old knees this Sabbath, giving grace on the first pew." He coughed, laughed weakly, then patted Alyssa's hand.

Alyssa laughed lightly, too. It felt so good, she almost cried. Uncle D stepped closer and took Captain Mac's other hand.

"You old bull walrus." He sniffed. "I told the doctors you were too ornery to kick the bucket yet. The children are fine, Mac, just fine."

Captain Mac blinked, then smiled softly at his granddaughter.

"I knew you'd talk again one day when you got things right in your heart. Did ye remember everything about that day, lassie? Everything?"

Alyssa nodded.

"Aye, I thought as much. I felt Robbie here today. He was in the room with me all the while. He told me it was time for me to let go of him and start payin' attention to the livin' folks around me. I've been neglectin' you, lass, I know it. But I'm not goin' to sell the wee horses or send you away. I was an old fool to say those things. I could never live alone in Scotland without you and Davy to chat with." He coughed again and squeezed his eyes shut as if a wave of pain had just passed over him. "I have a wee bit of a headache."

"I won't cause any more trouble, Grandpa, I promise."

"Posh, don't make a promise ye canna' keep. If ye dinna get into a wee bit o' trouble now and again, ye wouldn't be my Robbie's child. He was a stubborn one, just like you." He closed his eyes and sighed. "Just like you."

The doctor touched Alyssa's shoulder. "That's enough talking for now. Let him get some sleep. His vital signs are strong. He should be all right after a few days of rest."

After the doctor had examined Alyssa's throat and sprayed it again, she and Uncle D entered the waiting room. Dylan looked up and Ty jumped to his feet.

"Is he . . . ?"

"He pulled through. He'll be okay," Alyssa said.

"Good." Ty pretended to wipe his brow. Then his mouth opened wide. "What did you say?"

"I said—"

"You're talking!" He broke into her words. "You're really talking!"

Alyssa felt heat rush over her face. All of a sudden she didn't know what to say. It was tempting to go back into her shell of silence.

"Talking was the only way I could let my grandfather know I was alive," she said with a shrug.

Ty grabbed Alyssa's hand and shook it, then threw his arms around her and hugged tightly. He stepped back, squared his shoulders, and rubbed his nose.

"You're something else, Blondie."

Dylan quietly crept closer and stared into his sister's face. The last time she had spoken to him, he had been a happy little five-year-old playing with his plastic animals and toy cars on the living room floor. Now he was a serious-faced little man.

"I'm sorry for all the trouble you've been through," she said. "You're a brave kid." She tousled his curly brown hair. Flecks of dried mud fell to the floor.

Dylan shrugged his narrow shoulders. "It wasn't so bad."

Ty laughed, then punched Dylan lightly in the ribs. "Curly's braver than I was. He didn't complain or cry once. I was shaking in my boots."

Alyssa laughed, too. It was the first time in three years that she had felt laughter fill her stomach and roll up her throat and out her mouth. It felt too good for words.

"Do you think your grandfather's horses will be okay?" Ty asked.

Out of habit, Alyssa nodded.

"What?" Ty put his hand to his ear and cocked his head to one side. "I didn't hear you."

"Yes," Alyssa said in a firm, clear voice. "The horses will be okay. Say, I'm hungry, aren't you?"

The two boys agreed, so they got Uncle D

and ate in the hospital cafeteria. By the time they finished, the wind had almost stopped and the rain was hardly more than a gentle shower. They stepped outside and walked down the street to a Red Cross shelter. The night sky was partially clear, and the moon and several stars shone brightly between spotty clouds.

"I've always thought that the weather after a great storm is the most beautiful," Uncle D said as he drew in the cool, fresh air. "Now, you children get a good night's sleep. I want to leave early in the morning to check on my café to see if it's still standing. And you can check on Mac's horses."

"What about Aunt Melinda?" Dylan asked. "She'll be worried, won't she?"

"I'll get word to your aunt and uncle that you kids are okay as soon as I find a telephone that works."

Alyssa was tired and sore all over from paddling the lifeboat and from fighting Hurricane Berta, but she and Ty and Dylan played a couple of card games on the shelter floor before sleeping. Alyssa talked and talked until her voice got hoarse and her throat got sore again. When they finally said goodnight, she fell into the deepest and most peaceful sleep she had experienced for the past three years.

The next morning Uncle D woke everyone up before sunrise, eager to see about his café and house. After eating breakfast and checking on Captain Mac once more, they crossed the parking lot to the Jeep Cherokee.

How different the sky looked today. Gold and pink clouds radiated over the ocean like the wings of an unearthly bird of paradise. The soft rhythm of a gentle surf blended with the laughter of sea gulls. Alyssa stood in awe of the sea's beauty and breathed in the cool, pure air. She could not remember ever having seen a more beautiful morning.

As they opened the Jeep doors, a silver Mercedes pulled into the parking lot. When her aunt and uncle and cousin climbed out of their car, Alyssa's instincts told her to run. She knew her aunt's tongue could slash her. Yet another part of Alyssa told her to stand up to the woman hurrying toward them. With her newfound voice, she could tell Aunt Melinda what she thought. Alyssa trembled in anticipation of the confrontation about to begin.

By the time Aunt Melinda reached the Jeep, her face was crimson. Cecile dragged behind, her arm in a white plaster cast.

"Oh, Dylan!" Aunt Melinda said as she jerked

him close to her and squeezed with all her might. "We were so worried about you."

Uncle Steven put his hands on Alyssa's shoulders. "Uncle D told us what happened. Are you kids okay?"

Alyssa and Dylan nodded.

"It wasn't a very bright idea to go out in a hurricane, was it?" he teased, and chucked Alyssa on her chin.

"Well, it was mostly my fault," Ty quickly spoke up. "I asked them to visit me on my stepdaddy's shrimp boat. We were just going to stay a few minutes, but something happened. We ... well, we ended up on the sea and couldn't get back right away. It wasn't their fault."

"Dylan was on a shrimp boat? It's a wonder he didn't go into convulsions. Did the doctors give you some antihistamines?" Aunt Melinda asked.

Dylan shook his head and wiggled out of her arms.

"I don't want to take any medicine, Aunt Melinda. I'm not sick."

"Dylan was a real hero," Ty said. "Being on the boat didn't bother him. I think he liked the storm, didn't you, Curly?"

Dylan grinned up at Ty.

"It was fun. I only coughed a little bit. And I ate fish."

259

"You ate fish! Oh, no. I'm going to take you straight to the doctor. You might have an allergic reaction. Steven, we'd better hurry and get Dylan to the hospital." Her dark eyebrows twisted and she bit her lower lip.

"No!" Alyssa shouted, unable to bear another word from her aunt. "Leave my brother alone!" She pulled Dylan close and wrapped her arms around his shoulders. "He's not allergic to anything."

"Mommy! She's talking!" Cecile whispered.

"Alyssa!" Uncle Steven shook his head in disbelief. "Well, what do you know? After three years. That's wonderful." He reached down and patted her shoulder.

"I know what I'm talking about, Alyssa," Aunt Melinda said in a sharp voice, ignoring her husband and daughter. "I used to think my little Charlie wasn't allergic to anything. He was so healthy. So full of life. If I'd been more careful, more aware of the signs, he might still be alive today. I can't stand by and let it happen to Dylan. I can't—" Her voice broke and she quickly covered her mouth with a tissue.

"He's not going to die." Alyssa tried not to shout. "He's not little Charlie, Aunt Melinda. He's my brother—Dylan, son of the waves."

Alyssa glared at her aunt's face, watching it

slowly change. At first Alyssa thought the woman would scream, but as the seconds ticked away, a look she'd never seen before crept into the woman's eyes. For an instant, they reminded Alyssa of her mother's hazel eyes. Then Aunt Melinda released a long, slow breath. Tears gently fell down her flushed cheeks, then she openly wept into her tissue. Uncle Steven wrapped his arms around her trembling shoulders but didn't say a word.

After a few minutes she blew her nose and cleared her throat.

"Well, I *knew* you could talk if you put your mind to it, Alyssa," she said in a husky voice. "Thank goodness you finally came to your senses. But I still think you shouldn't have taken Dylan on the shrimp boat—"

"Aunt Melinda, Alyssa saved my life," Dylan's small voice broke in. "She took good care of me. She likes me. *You* hate me."

Aunt Melinda's eyes opened wide. For a moment she was speechless.

"I don't hate you, Dylan. Why would you say that? Why, you . . . you mean the world to me. Don't you realize that?"

"You're always making me go to the doctor and telling me I'm sick when I feel fine. I like to eat fish. Alyssa told me I used to eat it when I was a kid. I like to ride bikes and play in the ocean.

Why do you treat me like a baby? I don't want to live with you anymore! I hate you!"

Dylan jerked free from his sister's arms and ran toward the sea. Alyssa saw a sad, defeated look sweep over Aunt Melinda's face, and suddenly she felt sorry for her. Her brother was wrong about Aunt Melinda not liking him. She did take good care of him. If she just wouldn't be so scared that Dylan was going to die like little Charlie. But there was no doubt in Alyssa's mind that Aunt Melinda loved Dylan.

"Aunt Melinda," Alyssa said, "I'll go talk to Dylan. He didn't mean what he said. He's just upset about being in the hurricane. It was a long day and night for us."

Aunt Melinda sighed and nodded. "For us, too, Alyssa," she said in a weak voice. Her face looked different. Dark circles shaded her eyes, and her skin seemed drawn tight around her mouth, as if she had not slept much. She had probably been worried that Dylan was going to be killed like his parents. Alyssa still didn't think she liked her aunt too much, but she did feel sorry for her.

Alyssa trotted after Dylan and caught up with him at the beach. Clumps of seaweed and sea grapes and other small debris covered the once golden sands. Dylan stood with his face toward the rising sun, angrily tossing broken scallop shells into the sea.

"Dylan!" she shouted. He didn't turn around or stop throwing shells.

Alyssa picked up a round shell half buried by a clump of seaweed. Slowly she turned it over in her hand, examining a dark brown spot in its center.

"Do you know what kind of shell this is?" she asked.

Dylan glanced at it, then shrugged. "No."

"It's a shark eye. And that one over there is part of a pink conch. You're holding a scallop shell. This is a good time to look for seashells, after a big storm. We can spend hours collecting them, if you want. I'll teach you all the names, and you can start your own collection. Each kind of shell has its own story." She reached into her pocket and removed the oblong mouse cowrie. The sunlight bounced off its glossy speckled form. "You can have this one if you want. It's very rare to find one on Galveston Island."

"What about *her*? *She* probably won't let me touch the sand or the seashells. They're too dirty."

"Well, it is dirty. But I don't think Aunt Melinda would mind once she realizes that you aren't allergic to dirt and fish. She didn't want you to get sick, like her other little boy, Charlie, that's all. I think she's going to be easier to live with from now on. We just have to let her know how we feel about things and keep reminding her that you're not Charlie. You're Dylan, son of the waves, right?"

"Well . . ." Dylan paused. "Aunt Melinda is a great cook and takes me a lot of places. And I really like Uncle Steven. Maybe it wouldn't be so bad if you came to live with us. Are you?"

Alyssa felt a chill. She had not given much thought to that. She had been too worried about her grandfather's recovery.

"I don't know," she said. "Maybe I will and maybe I won't. I guess it depends on how Grandpa feels about things. I want to stay with him. But if I have to, I'll come live with you in Houston."

"I want to live with Grandpa, too," Dylan said. "Can't I come live here with you?"

"I'm not sure. Maybe you're better off with Uncle Steven and Aunt Melinda. They'll take good care of you. We'll just have to wait and see. Let's go back now. I think you ought to apologize to Aunt Melinda."

Alyssa took her brother's hand and led him back to the parking lot. All eyes were fixed on them as they walked up. Uncle Steven nodded again and grinned as if he were about to burst with pride. Aunt Melinda's face looked more tired than ever. She twisted the Kleenex in her hands as she anxiously watched Dylan approach. Alyssa nudged her brother with her elbow. He took a deep breath.

"You're okay, Aunt Melinda," he said. "You're a good cook and all that stuff. I'm sorry I yelled at you."

Aunt Melinda smiled and released a heavy sigh. "Oh, you are the sweetest child, sometimes." She hugged him. "And you're sweet, too, Alyssa. I really am very glad that you're able to speak again. So is Steven."

"How about some breakfast?" Uncle Steven asked. "You kids must be hungry."

"We've already eaten," Alyssa said. "We were about to go check on the horses when you drove up. Can Dylan come with us? I want to show him something."

Aunt Melinda reluctantly let go of Dylan. "All right, but please be careful. And if he starts coughing . . ." She paused, glanced at Uncle Steven, then forced a smile. "Well, maybe he'll be okay this time. Just avoid getting in the dirt, Dylan." She wiped the crumpled tissue across her forehead.

"Good for you," Uncle Steven said and squeezed his wife's hand.

Uncle D, Ty, Dylan, and Alyssa climbed into the Cherokee. As the car moved slowly down Seawall Boulevard, Alyssa surveyed the destruction. She knew she should have felt terrible—the stables and Captain Mac's house were probably smashed to pieces, and the horses might be hurt. But instead she felt as if it were the first day of spring and flowers were sprouting all over her mother's garden. She drew in a deep gulp of fresh air and could have sworn that she smelled roses.

The serene ocean, speckled with small whitecaps, gently caressed the granite boulders below the tall concrete seawall. From everywhere people had come out to look at the damage and the sea. They picked up boards, metal, tree limbs, and bricks and swept up broken glass. One man climbed a tall tree to fetch his garbage can.

Uncle D's little café was a mess, but it was still standing. Alyssa told him she wanted to walk to the pasture and stables. It was only a mile, and she wanted to take the opportunity to talk to Dylan and Ty. And talk they did. About everything and everyone. She called Ty a hero for rescuing her grandfather, and he insisted she was still the craziest girl he had ever met. Dylan had a lot of questions, too, about his early childhood, which he only vaguely remembered.

As soon as the stables came into sight, Ty broke

into a run and shouted at the top of his lungs for no apparent reason. Maybe he was just glad to be alive.

"Watch out for rattlesnakes!" Alyssa warned. "There may be some floating in the marshes and ditches."

Ty screamed hysterically and lifted his short legs high in the air in a crazy jig, making his companions break into laughter. Laughing felt so good to Alyssa, she ran after Ty, ignoring her own advice.

The beach looked clean and bare, except for some dead jellyfish and clumps of seaweed and driftwood. The sand dunes that once bordered the flat beach had been washed away, leaving only a few clumps of sea oats swaying by their long, exposed roots. The morning glories and railroad vines had been ripped up and blown away, too. The old tree trunk that Alyssa sat on every day was nowhere in sight. A lump rose to her throat as she thought about the many days she had spent sitting on it, watching the sea for her father to return. Now it seemed only appropriate that it was gone, for it was no longer needed.

Captain Mac's shack was drenched inside and out. Tree limbs and seaweed covered the porch steps. Windowpanes had shattered and part of the roof was gone, but the house was still there and so were the stables. The threesome picked their way through the soggy furniture and overturned table and chairs. Alyssa's room had fared better than the rest of the house because it only had one small window. Her seashells lay strewn on the floor, and hunks of driftwood covered the mattress. When she opened her closet, the cat Urican dashed out in a blur of gray, then leapt to the window and stared at the water.

Ty straightened furniture in the living room while Dylan picked up photos of his parents. Alyssa saw something black in a corner peeking from under a damp newspaper. She shook the paper and saw her grandfather's favorite record, the one of bagpipes playing "Amazing Grace." She wiped it off gently and placed it on the table. Everything that had happened to her was amazing, indeed, she thought.

At the stables, they cleared debris away from the door. Inside they stood amid piles of wet hay and overturned feed bins. Ty laughed and made jokes about oatmeal. His quips broke the silence that had fallen over them like a heavy blanket.

"Maybe your grandfather wouldn't mind if I visited the stables on weekends or after school now and then. I don't see how you can do all this by yourself." Ty pushed the toe of his sneaker into the sand, which was piled up more than a foot at the stable entryway.

"Grandpa wouldn't mind. He would be glad. He might even pay you some money when the business gets back on its feet. I've always thought that with some fresh paint and a new sign out front we could attract more customers. Maybe tie some balloons on the fence for kids and offer cold drinks and snacks. Or open a little barbecue stand. Maybe I could teach riding lessons. There are lots of ways to make money here with a little elbow grease. My grandfather just sort of let everything go to pot after my folks died. I guess I did, too."

"You're a real go-getter, Blondie. It'll be fun working with you. Do you wanna go look at the horses now?"

"Yes," Alyssa said as she picked up a tube of black salve. "I should put this on Stormy's neck so that cut won't get infected."

They trudged through water and mud until they reached the high pasture and the barn. Alyssa climbed the fence and whistled. Stormy neighed in reply. They checked out all of the horses. None of them were hurt, just wet and hungry. Alyssa gently rubbed the salve over Stormy's neck wound, which was not very serious.

"Do you want to tie them together and take

them back to the stables?" Ty asked as he stroked Stormy's neck.

Alyssa nodded. "Yes, but I have something to do first. If you don't mind, I want to show my little brother something. Alone."

Alyssa was deep in her own thoughts when Ty spoke. She didn't hear him and for a long time didn't speak. Ty cocked his head to one side and studied her face. "Hey, you're not going to go back into your cocoon, are you? I mean, you *are* going to keep on talking from now on, aren't you?"

Alyssa blinked, then smiled. "Of course. I made a promise to my grandfather and I have to keep it. But I have something to show Dylan. We have to say good-bye to someone."

"Sure," Ty said with a shrug. "I guess it's none of my business, anyhow."

Alyssa saw the hurt look in his blue eyes.

"Ty, thank you for . . . well, for everything," she said softly. "You saved my life, you know."

He shrugged again and looked at the ground. "Naw, I didn't. If there's one thing I learned from all this mess, it's that you sure can take care of yourself, Blondie."

"Well, I wasn't exactly talking about being in danger. Not physically. What I meant was that you helped me see things I'd been missing. Things about my grandfather and my parents. And things about my little brother. Anyway, thanks." She threw her arms around his sturdy neck and squeezed with all her might.

Ty rubbed his nose and squared his shoulders. "You're all right, Blondie," he said as a grin spread across his face. "Don't worry about these horses. I'll have them all rounded up by the time you two get back."

Alyssa took Dylan's hand into hers. "Dylan, let's ride Stormy over to a special place I want to show you. I won't let him buck or run."

Dylan didn't hesitate. He stepped into her cupped hands and swung up onto Stormy's back. She slid up behind him.

"I used to ride horses when I was a little kid, didn't I?" he asked.

'You sure did. And you swam in the ocean and played in the sand."

"And I ate fish?"

"Yes, you ate fish. You even caught a fish once. Daddy showed you how."

They rode toward the secret cove where she had tied the green boat. Most of the reeds and grasses of the marsh flats were still underwater. The great blue heron that usually screamed at her from the fence post was perched in a treetop, looking confused.

At first Alyssa couldn't find the green skiff.

She saw the tall cottonwood tree, but it didn't seem in the right place and it leaned to one side. But it was the only tall tree standing, so she dismounted and waded to it. She ran her hands underwater along the tree trunk until she felt the rope. She pulled it slowly until, with a great gurgle, the green prow emerged from the murky brown water.

With Dylan's help she unfastened the towrope and turned the boat sideways to empty part of the water. They dragged it to land, then turned it over and drained out the rest of the water, mud, and debris, including two crabs and a fish.

"Whose boat is this?" Dylan asked.

"It's mine. But now it's yours, too. Our father made it with his own hands for my tenth birthday. And he was going to make one for you when you turned ten."

Dylan studied the boat.

"Our father was a nice man, wasn't he?"

"Yes, he was," Alyssa replied. She dragged the boat to the shore, helped Dylan step into it, then carefully pushed it into the water. She used a long piece of tree limb as a pole to push away from the bank. Standing up, she gently poled the skiff out of the cove into West Bay. The water was smooth and calm, even though it was higher than usual.

As Alyssa steered the boat, she told Dylan about flounders and redfish and stingrays. She told him about the day their father had sat in the lap of a beautiful actress while she rode a horse down the beach. She told him about the day their father's baseball team won the state championship, and how his laugh sounded. Then she told Dylan about their mother's garden and her green thumb, and how the wind blew her long blond hair back from her face when she sailed on the ocean. She told him all this as they watched the sun climb above the island, its rays bouncing off the white wings of laughing sea gulls.

When Alyssa stopped talking for a moment, Dylan turned to her with a serious look on his face.

"Alyssa, am I going to come live with you and Grandpa?"

"I truly don't know. Maybe I will come to live with you. Or maybe we'll all move to Scotland. Who can say? But whatever happens, the important thing is that we will be together from now on."

"Aunt Melinda said you . . ." He paused as he struggled with the words. "She said you stopped talking because you saw something terrible happen to our mother and father. Was it? Was it terrible?"

Alyssa swallowed hard, forcing a sharp lump down.

"Yes, it was terrible, but that wasn't the reason I stopped talking. I made a promise to our father that I would be quiet, and he made a promise that he would join me later. But now I know he's never coming back."

"Our father lied?"

"It wasn't exactly a lie. He only broke his promise because he had to. Just like I had to break my promise to save Grandpa. Sometimes it just happens that way, and it's nobody's fault. I should have known that, but I was just a child."

Alyssa felt hot tears falling down her cheeks and heard her voice turn husky. Then she felt Dylan's small, warm hand slip inside hers.

They sat in the green skiff looking across the bay. Cars crept over the causeway as people returned to the island. Far to the northeast they saw the last dark clouds and dying rage of Hurricane Berta.

Alyssa thought of Captain Mac's and Uncle D's tall tales of sailors lost at sea in great storms. She thought of her foolish childhood dreams of dancing with *Urican*, the devil wind that swept across the Caribbean. She could have hated that angry, swirling mass of water and wind and waves for tearing families apart. But it wasn't hatred she felt as she took a long, deep breath of fresh air and turned the boat around. For this time that devil wind had brought a family back together. They weren't as whole as they had once been, but they would survive.